11/06

The Legend of the Wandering King

LAURA GALLEGO GARCÍA
Translated by Dan Bellm

ARTHUR A. LEVINE BOOKS

AN IMPRINT OF SCHOLASTIC INC.

Text copyright © 2002 by Laura Gallego García
Translation copyright © 2005 by Dan Bellm
All rights reserved. Published by Arthur A. Levine Books, an imprint of Scholastic Inc.,
Publishers since 1920, by arrangement with Ediciones SM, Madrid, Spain.

SCHOLASTIC and the LANTERN LOGO are trademarks
and/or registered trademarks of Scholastic Inc.

Library of Congress Cataloging-in-Publication Data

Gallego García, Laura, 1977–
[Leyenda del rey errante. English]
The legend of the Wandering King / by Laura Gallego García ;
translated by Dan Bellm. — 1st ed.   p. cm.
Summary: Motivated by jealousy and the desire to receive acclaim as a great poet,
Walid ibn Hujr, a prince of ancient Arabia, commits acts which completely
change the course of his life.

ISBN 0-439-58556-2

[1. Conduct of life — Fiction.   2. Fate and fatalism — Fiction.   3. Choice — Fiction.   4.
Poetry — Fiction.   5. Kings, queens, rulers, etc. — Fiction.   6. Arabian Peninsula — Fiction.]
I. Bellm, Dan. II. Title.   PZ7.G155625Le 2005   [Fic] — dc22   2004011696

10 9 8 7 6 5 4 3 2   05 06 07 08 09

Printed in the United States of America   23
First American edition, August 2005

Submitted excerpt from p. 21, used as epigraph, from WARRIOR OF THE LIGHT:
A MANUAL by PAULO COELHO Copyright © 2003 by Paulo Coelho.
Reprinted by permission of HarperCollins Publishers Inc.

*Thanks to Professor Philip F. Kennedy of New York University for his advice
on Arabian history and Arabic translation and transliteration, and to William Newton
of the University of Texas and Professor William Granara of Harvard University
for their help with Arabic pronunciation.*

Acknowledgments

To Professor Josefina Veglison, whose Arabic literature classes, full of stories and legends about the mythic pre-Islamic poets, inspired me in part to write this book. I am also grateful for the help of her magnificent anthology, *La poesía arabe clásica*, the source of the quotations from classical Arab poets that I have included in the novel, and I apologize for any liberties I have taken in using these legends in my own way.

To Andrés, for listening patiently as I worked out this story, for helping me throughout the creative process, and for inspiring me with the figure of the man in the red turban.

To Guillermo, for his gift of a great idea for the ending of the book, which was hobbling along until he arrived to put things right.

For the secondary school student at the Colegio María Inmaculada de Puerto Sagunto, who, in a conversation about my novel *Finis Mundi*, asked me: *How can they see the future by using the Axes of Time, if the future is something we create ourselves?* Recalling this question I didn't know how to answer, I recognize my error now, and I've tried to correct it with this book.

To my parents, for bringing me back from their travels an authentic Turkish carpet. Surely it has brought me good luck!

To my brother Sergio, for being the first to read this book and for attacking it so mercilessly (just kidding).

And last but not least, to Nuria, for also reading the earliest draft, for helping me see the possibilities in it, and for catching various mistakes that slipped past me.

To all of you, thanks again.

CONTENTS

Every Warrior of the Light has, at sometime in the past, lied to and betrayed someone.

Every Warrior of the Light has trodden a path that was not his. . . .

Every Warrior of the Light has, at least once, believed that he was not a Warrior of the Light. . . .

That is why he is a Warrior of the Light: because he has been through all this and yet has never lost hope of being better than he is.

— Paulo Coelho,
Warrior of the Light: A Manual

Before the days of Mohammed and Islam, Arabia was a land of mystery and legend. In that era, which the Arabs call jahiliyya, or "the time of ignorance," everything was possible, because the only rules of behavior were those of honor and love — and honor and love break all the rules. In those days, a city was barely a large-sized village beside an oasis. The primal spirits of the desert, called djinns, could catch an unwary traveler by surprise around any bend. The whole earth possessed a special magic. And every Arab was a poet at heart.

In those mythical days there lived a man of whom nothing remains but jumbled fragments of legend, a man who set out on an epic search and came to be called the Wandering King. This is his story.

Prologue

THE CONDEMNED MAN

The *suluk* dismounted with a graceful leap and unsheathed his sword. But Walid made no move to defend himself; he stood calm and still and waited for death.

"I swore that I would kill you if you crossed my path again," the *suluk* said.

"I remember," said Walid, "and I accept my fate."

The other paused. "I hardly know what to call you. Are you brave, or are you now completely mad?"

"Perhaps I am both," Walid answered.

The *suluk* did not reply, but raised his sword above his motionless opponent.

Their eyes met, and in the horseman's gaze there was a steely flash that Walid knew very well. The sword blade shone a moment in the blazing desert sun.

Then Walid saw the sword descend toward him and sink into his chest. As he fell to the sand, clasping the bloody wound, his life passed again before his eyes. Once more he saw the place where he had been born and spent his youth: a high-walled palace in Dhat Kahal, the city of seven towers — a small refuge of green in the middle of a seemingly endless desert; the palace where his glory and legend and shame had taken shape and grown. . . .

1

THE PRINCE

Everyone said that Walid ibn Hujr, prince of Kinda, had been touched by a *djinn* at the moment of his birth. Handsome of body and fair of soul, generous as a rush of water, he never held back his gifts when it came to pleasing his beloved people, whom he treated with magnanimity and justice. At the age of seventeen, he was a perfect courtier, gracious and elegant, fluent in several tongues, and blessed with remarkable tact and diplomacy. Whether serving abroad as an ambassador or hosting emissaries from far-off lands, Walid ibn Hujr managed his political duties with a fine and subtle skill.

And his skills at war? He mounted a horse as if he'd been born for that purpose, and his talent with a sword was legendary. When it came to defending his land from plunderers or the warriors of rival kingdoms, he could cross the desert on horseback like a ray of light in the starry sky. Anyone who had seen him in the pitch of battle said that Walid was like a lion, magnificent and untamable.

The prince of Kinda was young, poised, gallant, generous, witty, intelligent, brave, and skilled at war, but he was also a man of culture. All of his gifts had created in him an insatiable desire for knowledge, and Walid ibn Hujr learned to read and write in an era when this was still uncommon, collecting an impressive palace library that he visited as often as his courtly duties allowed.

These qualities stirred great pride in his father, the old King Hujr, and his subjects, the people of Kinda, said, "Truly, our prince has been inspired by the *djinns* of the desert."

But even with these gifts, Walid ibn Hujr aspired to one thing more than any other. He wanted to be a great poet.

And so the prince appeared before the king one day, bowed respectfully, and asked permission to take leave of the kingdom for several weeks.

"Why, my son?" said the king.

Walid ibn Hujr raised his head proudly. His father had lost his sight some time ago, yet he could not help but catch the excited tone in his son's voice when he answered:

"I want to attend the annual competition in Ukaz."

King Hujr raised an eyebrow but paused a moment before replying. When he did, his tone was rather sharp.

"Not only to *attend* but to *take part*, you mean?"

"Father, you know I am a good poet."

When the king did not answer, Walid went on:

"The greatest poets in the world gather every year in Ukaz, Father, and the winner is granted the honor of having his *qasida* embroidered in gold letters on silk and hung from the veils of the temple of Kaaba. I . . ."

"I know very well that you covet that honor," the king interrupted. "And it's good that you seek to exalt the name of your people. Such a desire is to your credit, Walid. Pride is a great quality of our tribe."

The king paused, and the prince waited, holding his breath.

"But as you have said yourself," the king went on, "the most renowned poets in the world gather in Ukaz. You might end up in disgrace, my son, and you are not some anonymous young man: You are the heir to the throne of Kinda."

"So, then . . . ?"

"I will grant you permission to take part in that contest when you have proven yourself the greatest poet in *this* kingdom, and not until then."

There was a moment of silence. Outside the palace, the wind tossed the leaves of the palm trees, and the king turned his head to listen. Walid knew his father loved this sound, so he waited cautiously before asking:

"And how will I prove that, Father?"

The king was quiet for a moment, then raised his head and said:

"Organize your own competition. Bring judges from other lands, impartial judges, and offer a generous and tempting prize. When you hear the winner's name from the judges' lips and it is yours, son, you will have my permission to go to Ukaz."

The prince said nothing, but he had turned pale. He had no doubt that he could win such a contest, but organizing it meant delaying his journey to Ukaz for another year. Still, he owed it to his father to obey, and he knew him well enough to realize that nothing would change his mind.

Muttering a few words of formality, Walid ibn Hujr bowed again before the king of Kinda and left the room.

* * *

Soon it became known throughout the land that Prince Walid was calling all poets to a great competition of *qasidas*, for which the prize would be a bag of gold. The news spread quickly, even beyond the borders of Kinda, running from one village to another and crossing the desert with the merchant caravans. Walid had to combine the task of organizing the competition with all his other affairs of state.

Within his own literary circle there was talk of nothing

else. All the young poets and courtiers were filled with excitement when Walid announced that none other than the famous poet al-Nabiga al-Dubyani would preside over the panel of judges. His verses reigned supreme in all of Arabia; all agreed that this great man would grant the victory to Prince Walid, because there was no greater poet in Kinda.

Walid listened to their praise with a smile. It was good to know that everyone in Kinda thought as his friends did.

* * *

The sun rose brightly over Kinda on the day of the competition. Dhat Kahal, the kingdom's proud capital, was bustling with humanity; the news had swept through Arabia like a stormy desert wind, and Arabs are a people very fond of poetry. Outside the city walls crowned with seven towers a multitude was camped: Bedouins, visitors from other villages, even caravans whose guides had changed their routes just to be present for this great event. Along with merchants, foreigners, ruffians, and a general assortment of curious folk, *rawis* of every type and rank could be seen here and there. These were reciters of poetry who aspired to compose verses of their own one day, but contented themselves meanwhile with declaiming the latest *qasidas* composed by their masters, whom they were obliged to represent before the members of the jury in this poetry contest.

In the plaza where market days were usually held, a platform had been built and covered with canvas to protect it from the relentless Arabian sun. Although the seats reserved for the judges were still empty, as were those on the grand dais where the king, his two wives, and Walid his heir and prince would sit, a small crowd had already gathered in the plaza, seeking out a bit of ground where they could settle themselves.

"I don't know why there's such a commotion," one woman snorted, trying to cut a path through the crowd to the other side of the plaza. "The prince is going to win, and everyone knows it. He's the best."

"But what if he *doesn't* win?" muttered a boy who happened to overhear.

"But he *will* win," the woman insisted.

"Yes, I know, I know . . . but . . . what if he doesn't?"

Perhaps it was this mystery that had attracted most of the crowd, and while many others had come to the plaza out of a pure love of poetry, even they must have asked themselves such a question over the course of the morning.

Finally, when the plaza was bursting to overflowing, the judges appeared and ascended the platform one by one.

There were five: one from the fierce land of Syria, one from the refined land of Persia, a third from lovely

Palmyra, and the next from the palaces of Egypt, where he sang of the glories of the pharaohs' successors. All had come in answer to the call of the noble prince of Kinda.

The fifth was an Arab, and the crowd accorded him a respectful silence. This was al-Nabiga al-Dubyani, the greatest poet of his time, who served as the court poet of al-Hira and who, some time before, had composed a *mu'allaqa*, a *qasida* honored by being embroidered in gold letters on silk and hung from the veils of the temple of Kaaba, having triumphed in the competition of Ukaz.

Since he was the sole Arab on the jury, he was charged with judging not only the beauty of the competing *qasidas* but also their perfection of form. Even if the others knew the language perfectly well and could judge a poem's artistry, only al-Nabiga grasped the technical details of creating a perfect *qasida*.

The five judges took their places but remained standing, because the royal family had just entered the plaza. Protected by a detachment of guards, King Hujr, his oldest son, and the grand vizier all rose to the dais, followed by the king's two wives and their servants.

When all had taken their seats, the king turned to face the crowd in the plaza and spoke a few words. His speech was not long or flowery; King Hujr had never been a poet, nor was he as eloquent as his son. Kinda was a small kingdom, made up of one city, three or four villages, six or seven nomadic tribes, and a stretch of desert. It was Prince Walid who had been forming, little by little, an elegant and cultured life at court. His political skills had caused merchant caravans from the East to pass more often through Kinda; his diplomatic efforts had made the kingdom something more than the loose confederation of tribes it had been when his father, King Hujr, had taken the throne.

But the old, blind king still considered himself a man of the desert. And so he finished his speech and yielded the stage to the great poet who would preside over the judges in the competition.

Al-Nabiga al-Dubyani smiled and bowed with reverence before the king of Kinda.

"I am grateful from the bottom of my heart for your kind words, sire," he said, "but I fear I do not deserve them. If it is my poems that have brought me here, I give thanks for that. But today it is not I who must recite poems, and therefore, let us take no more time away from the true heroes of this contest of poetry." And with these words, he turned toward the secretary and signaled that the competition could begin.

Some in the crowd murmured in disappointment; most had expected that al-Nabiga would treat them to one of his supremely beautiful *qasidas*. But there was no time for complaint, because at once the secretary announced the first name, and the first contestant rose to the stage.

The rules of the competition dictated that the poets' *rawis* would recite their *qasidas* for them. In this way, the contest became almost anonymous, although everyone knew Prince Walid's *rawi*, Hakim, a thin, long-faced young man who had often shown himself worthy of his post, thanks to his powerful memory and his clear, calm voice.

The first *rawi*, perhaps because he was the first, or because he was very young, went astray several times, and got tongue-tied, and failed to make his voice carry strongly enough, to the great despair of his master, who groaned in frustration behind the scenes. But for all that, the *qasida* was beautiful; perhaps the judges would not penalize the poor poet too much for having a somewhat incompetent reciter.

The contestants kept coming forward, one by one. The crowd applauded each *qasida* as if it were unique in its beauty, because each was. Although many had come just to see the prince make off with the victory, none could help but feel entranced by the magic of words. And then the secretary announced:

"Amir ibn Hammad!"

At once, a very young *rawi*, perhaps eleven years old, leaped to the stage and saluted the judges with a self-assured bow. He was slender, dark-skinned, and sprightly, and some were unable to stifle a guffaw when they saw him. He was wearing a threadbare and faded *djellabah*, but he displayed a dazzling smile.

"Are you ready, son?" al-Nabiga al-Dubyani asked him in a friendly tone.

Amir ibn Hammad nodded without losing his enchanting smile. Then he began to recite the *qasida* in a voice that was strong, clear, pure, and profoundly moving.

The first part of a *qasida*, the *nasib*, customarily tells of the poet arriving at an empty encampment to find that his beloved has gone away, perhaps forever. Many poets had described such a scene before, since it is repeated in every *qasida* worthy of the name, and often with incomparable beauty. And yet, at that moment, no one witnessing the competition of Kinda could remember having heard such love and desolation depicted in the words of a poem. On the lips of Amir ibn Hammad, the poet's beloved became much more than a beautiful woman; she came to life. Some members of the jury could not help but tremble; if such was the sound of these verses in a young boy's mouth, how might they sound on the lips of the poet who had written them?

At the appropriate time, Amir passed on to the second part of the *qasida*, the *rahil*, the poet's journey across the desert. It was no less beautiful than the part before: The words of the poem left the young boy's lips and floated above the plaza, forming in the minds of his listeners a landscape so alive and real that it seemed they could smell the desert and feel on their skin the coolness of an Arabian night on the dunes.

At last, the boy turned to the *madih*, the simplest, or most difficult, part of the *qasida*. Simple, because it usually consisted of an homage to some important person, and difficult because there was nothing that poets hadn't said before in praise of their benefactors; it was almost impossible to be original. This was why many poets chose to write *fakhrs* instead — songs of self-praise extolling their own virtues as people or warriors or poets, or those of their tribe or clan.

But the verse that Amir recited was not a *fakhr*; it was a warm and tender homage to King Hujr, and it sounded completely different from everything that court poets had written before. Far from using excessive hyperbole, the simplicity and sincerity with which it praised King Hujr's generous nature became moving in some strange new way, taking a living shape, as if these were much more than beautiful words.

At last, after the final verse had left his lips with the lightness of a dove, Amir's voice fell silent, and a hush descended over the plaza. Then everyone erupted into cheers for Amir, who turned toward the crowd and offered an elegant bow.

On the royal dais, King Hujr smiled, but the prince seemed pale and troubled.

The boy leaped from the stage and disappeared into the crowd.

The contest went on, and one after another, the

participants' *rawis* ascended the platform to recite their *qasidas*, but all of them sounded cold and lifeless after the poem that Amir ibn Hammad had spoken.

Nevertheless, the magic of those words disappeared from the plaza after a while, even if a bit of it remained in everyone's hearts. Most of the crowd now waited for Hakim, the *rawi* of Prince Walid, to play his part. The prince had regained his usual confident expression, smiling and applauding each *qasida* generously.

At last the secretary pronounced Hakim's name, and he ascended the stage with a complacent smile. He and the prince exchanged a knowing look, and the *rawi* nodded almost imperceptibly. He was well aware of what he needed to do.

The *qasida* of Prince Walid was very beautiful, a work of uncommon perfection and loveliness. The crowd listened to it in silence, and when Hakim had finished reciting, everyone answered his performance with heartfelt cheers and applause.

Prince Walid's poem concluded the competition. The judges retired to deliberate. Murmurs and comments were heard in the crowd:

"What did I tell you? The prince is going to win!"

"If everyone knew it already, why organize a contest at all?"

"But there was another *qasida* that was truly beautiful. . . ."

Still, Prince Walid smiled as he spoke quietly with the vizier.

The debate among the judges seemed to take forever. Finally, al-Nabiga al-Dubyani rose and turned to face King Hujr. Bowing respectfully toward him, he spoke three words to the king, privately, in a low voice. Just three words.

The king's face remained impassive as he rose and announced in a voice that echoed throughout the plaza:

"Amir ibn Hammad!"

2

THE JUDGE

Silence fell, the prince turned deathly pale, and everyone stared at the king and the jury as if they could not
believe what they had heard.

Only one person reacted to the surprising announcement: A thin and somewhat ragged boy made his way
through the crowd and placed himself before the royal
dais. Many recognized him at once as the boy who had
recited that beautiful *qasida*: Amir ibn Hammad, was it?
Most of the crowd had already forgotten his name.

The boy was leading by the hand an equally ragged
man, who walked awkwardly, his head bowed, trying to
cover his face with his turban as much as he could.

"Sire, the winning *rawi* has arrived," the vizier told
the king in a low voice. "He's a little boy . . ."

The king nodded. "You are Amir ibn Hammad?" he
asked.

"Yes, sire," he answered.

"Who is your master?"

The man standing next to him moved forward, made an awkward bow before the king, and blushing deeply, said:

"I am, your majesty. I am his father. My name is Hammad ibn al-Haddad."

"Very well, Hammad ibn al-Haddad," said the king, raising his voice so that all could hear. "The judges of this competition have declared that your *qasida* has carried the day. You have therefore won the prize of a bag of gold."

His tone of voice remained absolutely neutral; not for a moment did he seem disappointed by his son's loss or make the slightest gesture toward him. The prince remained stupefied. Bug-eyed and blanched, his face had lost much of its beauty.

"I . . . I . . ." Hammad stuttered. "It . . . is an honor. . . ." And he made another bow.

With trembling hands he grasped the bag of gold, and the crowd remained silent until someone shouted:

"Long live Hammad ibn al-Haddad!"

Many others now joined in: "Long live the victor! Long live Hammad ibn al-Haddad!"

The entire plaza erupted in a burst of cheers and applause, and during the outcry King Hujr leaned toward his vizier, who rushed to his side, saying, "Yes, your majesty?"

"Make sure that this man arrives home safely, and

that no one tries to attack him on the way. He is carrying a veritable fortune."

"Yes, your majesty."

The prince remained lost in thought, saying not a word. The king turned toward him:

"We must be thankful to Hammad for coming to our competition," he said curtly. "He spared us a far greater disaster. Better to be made a fool of here than in Ukaz, don't you agree?"

Walid did not answer, only moving when his *rawi* Hakim appeared unobtrusively beside him. Then he lifted his head and searched the multitude for the beaming winner of the prize, lost now in the crowd.

"Search for him," he whispered to Hakim. "Search for him, and find out who he is."

Hakim nodded and left the royal platform, silent as a shadow.

❈   ❈   ❈

"He's just some poor devil, sire," said the *rawi*. "The prize has given him more wealth than he's seen in his whole life. I doubt that he will ever return for this competition."

"And yet, you can't be sure."

They were in the prince's chambers, and Walid was

pacing nervously from one end of the room to the other. Hakim, standing by the door, chose to remain silent after hearing this reply. He knew his lord and master's moods very well.

"You didn't manage to find him," said Walid with a frown.

"He left as quickly and as quietly as he came," Hakim answered smoothly. "He didn't stay the night in the city. It appears that your noble and excellent father's private guard escorted him home. If you desire, I can make some inquiries and . . ."

Walid raised a hand, and the *rawi* stopped speaking.

"No," said the prince. "My father would be suspicious, and having lost the competition, I've fallen somewhat out of his favor. . . ."

The chamber was silent but for the prince's nervous pacing. Hakim waited impassively.

"Perhaps you are right after all," Walid said at last. "He did not appear to be an ambitious man, just some simple wretch. If we hold the competition again next year, perhaps he won't come. . . ."

Hakim only bowed his head slightly.

"And then," the prince added, "the victory will be mine. No one will be able to deny that I am the greatest poet in Kinda: It will be my *qasida* that everyone remembers, not some ragged peasant's clumsy verses."

Hakim did not disagree, but he noticed that the prince had left unmentioned his old dream of taking part in the competition of Ukaz.

*   *   *

The months passed quickly. Walid continued to be a fine prince, attentive, generous, and brave, and soon put out of his mind his humiliating defeat at the hands of the unknown Hammad. By the time the announcement of another competition circulated throughout Kinda, people had become convinced that last year's results could only have been a mistake, due to some momentary confusion among the judges. Prince Walid was the greatest poet in the kingdom, and the memory of his glorious verses would live forever.

And so, on the morning of the contest, lovers of poetry and the merely curious all gathered once more in the market square of Dhat Kahal, mingling with the participating poets and their *rawis*. All had been arranged in the same way as the year before; why change anything? The same platform for the panel of judges, the same royal dais for the king and his family. The judges were also the same: one from Syria, one from Persia, one from Egypt, one from Palmyra, and the fifth was al-Nabiga al-Dubyani.

Prince Walid observed them gravely from his seat on the dais. Only he and the king knew that he had tried to bring in different judges, but his father had been absolutely inflexible in this matter: This jury had shown the year before that it could be impartial even to the prince who had invited them, and this was a quality the king valued above all else. This was no ordinary contest, as both of them knew. It was a test that the king had set for his son to prove that he could measure up to his dreams. In Walid's opinion, it was a harsh and unnecessary test, and it had turned out to be much more complicated than either of them had first imagined. But the king was stubborn, and his son was not without pride.

And so they had gathered again, one year later, and all would be the same as before.

The only unknown was Hammad ibn al-Haddad. No one knew whether he would return to compete, since the list of participants was held by the secretary and the judges, and they had scrupulously kept it secret. And if Hammad presented himself once again, would he manage to deny Walid the victory a second time?

The opening speeches came and went, in almost exactly the same words as the year before. Hardly anyone paid attention. Many kept looking around on the slightest pretext for any sign of Hammad or his son, the young *rawi* Amir. But neither one of them seemed to be present.

And so the competition began. This time, in a change of strategy, Walid had managed to make his *rawi* Hakim the first to take the stage.

The *qasida* that he recited was even more beautiful than the one of the year before; no one dared say a word or make the slightest sound while Hakim's voice echoed through the plaza, but many cast frequent glances toward the dais where Prince Walid was sitting. He displayed great serenity as he listened to the verses he himself had written, praising in song the beauty of women, the beauty of the desert, and the beauty of his lord and protector's soul, none other than that of his own father, King Hujr.

When Hakim finished reciting, the entire plaza cheered him as they had cheered for Hammad the year before. Walid let out a small, complacent smile, feeling utterly assured of victory.

The competition went on. *Rawis* of all classes and backgrounds and ages filed before the judges. The *qasidas* they recited were beautiful, but they cast no shadow on the radiantly perfect poem that Prince Walid had written.

When the sun was high and all had concluded that Walid would be the winner, the name of the last *rawi* was heard in the plaza:

"Amir ibn Hammad!"

Many did not recognize the name, and some had not even heard it. But for Prince Walid, up on the dais, those three words meant that his worst fears had come true, embodied in the figure of the boy who now jumped to the stage.

At once the plaza filled with murmurs of surprise:

"Look! Isn't that . . . ?"

"Yes, I think it's . . ."

"The one from last year!"

"Do you mean . . . "

"It's the *rawi* of that poet who won the prize!"

Walid gripped his seat; he had almost leaped up when he heard the name. He bit his lip and tried to appear calm. He didn't want anyone to think that he lacked confidence in his victory.

He observed the boy carefully. Yes, this was the one. He had grown a bit, and seemed better dressed than the year before, though his clothing remained extremely humble. But he still had that determined air and that glow of confidence. *He will grow up to be a brave man,* the prince suddenly thought. But at once he drove such thoughts from his head, because the boy had begun to recite his *qasida.*

Once more the *nasib* was full of life, its words bringing to the minds of its listeners images of a woman beyond compare, absolutely real, much more than an empty figure or a vague ideal. Once more the journey through the desert was painted with such poignant beauty that one could almost touch it with the fingertips. Once more the words of gratitude to the sovereign of Kinda were brimming with emotion, bringing tears to King Hujr's sightless eyes.

[23]

It seemed impossible to achieve more beauty than Hammad had formed into last year's *qasida* by repeating the very same themes, and yet he had done it. Everyone who was present that day could sense that words had a mysterious magical power, that they could reach the heart and make the oldest things new again, over and over, if only one used them with feeling and passion. And once they understood this, they never forgot it.

When Amir fell silent, the secretary announced that he had been the last contestant, and that the jury would now retire to make its decision. The crowd was in confusion, and so was Walid. From the second line that the boy had recited, he knew he had once again lost the competition.

He barely heard the confirmation of these fears from the mouth of al-Nabiga, and he barely saw the ungainly figure of Hammad ibn al-Haddad ascending the stage to receive his prize, looking even more afflicted than he had before, if such a thing was possible. Nor did the prince notice Hakim discreetly leaving his side in order to carry out the mission he had left unfinished one year ago.

"Let us return to the palace," said King Hujr, and Walid came back to the present moment. He sensed a weariness and disappointment in his father's voice, which pained him more than the curtness and tension of the previous time.

"I would like to have a few words with the master, if you will allow me, Father."

The king had no objection, and the prince approached the president of the jury, who was stepping down from the stage.

"Would you allow me a few minutes, master?" he asked. His voice was drowned out by the cheering in honor of Hammad, but al-Nabiga al-Dubyani looked at him with deep understanding, as if Walid's question were written on his face.

"By all means, noble prince," he said gently.

Soon they found themselves in a drawing room of the palace, fanned by a cool breeze.

"Great master, I . . ." Walid began.

"You want to know why a *qasida* as perfect as your own hasn't taken the prize," al-Nabiga finished for him.

Walid struggled not to seem too troubled or distraught.

"Naturally, I knew that it was perfect," he responded in a cold and haughty tone. "It must have been the boy's charm that swayed the jury."

Al-Nabiga shook his head.

"Sire, with all respect, the boy's charm had nothing to do with it. There are other reasons that more than justify the judges' decision."

"Explain them to me, then."

"The art of poetry is an ancient one, noble prince. The *qasida*, our most illustrious form of verse, is also the most complex, because of the many rules that . . ."

"I know," the prince cut in abruptly.

"Then you know that its form and its subject matter have not changed for centuries. With good reason a poet himself once asked, 'Have the poets left us anything to say, or can we only stammer as we find our way?'"

Al-Nabiga paused a moment. Walid was listening with an impassive expression.

"It seemed impossible to achieve a *qasida* more perfect than your own, my prince," the master concluded. "And yet that man has done it."

"But how?"

"By giving the poor old *qasida* something new: To its formal beauty he added an inner beauty of his own. Last year, we judges saw that something was missing in your *qasida* when we compared it with his. It was most evident in the *nasib*, although we could not say precisely what it was. Believe me, sire, I have pondered this question long and hard ever since, and I reached the conclusion that your verses were beautiful but lacking in substance. While Hammad's *nasib* was bursting with love, yours showed that you have never loved a woman."

"But I have loved *many* women," Walid objected.

Al-Nabiga nodded, as if he had expected such an answer.

"On that occasion, we decided to overlook this defect," he went on, "since it is common for poets to talk of things they know nothing of, and because you are young, but we found the same fault with your *rahil*: The desert as you described it seemed unreal; the dunes, the wind, the camels and jackals, the sky — it all seemed to have come from your head and not your heart, as if you had never crossed the desert that surrounds your city."

"But that's absurd!" the prince muttered. "I've captained dozens of expeditions!"

"Hammad surpassed you in this as well," al-Nabiga continued. "All of the judges agreed that this was a great poet who might revolutionize the poetry of the Arab world, simply by adding a basic element that so few poets before him had kept in mind."

"And what is that?"

"The heart," said al-Nabiga, giving the prince a long and searching look. "In the first competition, we judges were willing to overlook the *rahil* as well, for surely you would have no trouble surpassing Hammad in the *madih*. After all, you were both praising the same person, and how would Hammad love King Hujr more than you do, who are his firstborn son?"

Walid said nothing, and he kept silent for a long time after the great poet had gone away, stirring only when he heard someone in the doorway discreetly clear his throat.

Hakim had arrived.

3

THE CARPET WEAVER

"His name, as you know, is Hammad ibn al-Haddad,"
the *rawi* reported. "He lives in the oasis of al-Lakik and
works as a carpet weaver."

"Carpets?" repeated Walid, interrupting his nervous
pacing from one end of the room to the other. "Some
kind of merchant, I suppose."

"No, sire. To tell the truth, he earns all but nothing
from his carpets because he charges so little for them,
beautiful as they are."

"An impoverished peasant, and stupid, too," Walid
grunted. "But now he's become rich, thanks to the prize
of gold."

Hakim shook his head again.

"No, it appears that he has gone on living the same
simple life."

"Then how has he spent the money?" Walid asked in
a loud voice, resuming his pacing.

"He must have been burdened with debt," the *rawi* suggested. "And if he settled it all with last year's winnings, he'll be swimming in riches soon enough with the gold he's carried off this time."

Walid observed how bitterly Hakim spoke.

"The gold means nothing to me," the prince said. "There is plenty more in the royal coffers. What disturbs me is that he has snatched away a victory that should have been mine."

He paused at the window to look out at the desert lying beyond the walled city of Dhat Kahal and its seven towers. The sun set on the horizon, lighting the dunes with red and gold fire, but Walid was too preoccupied to appreciate its beauty.

"If you clear him out of your way," suggested Hakim, "surely the victory will be yours next year."

"No, that's no good. In the first place, my father will be suspicious if this . . . carpet weaver dies under strange circumstances. Not to mention, what good would it do to win if he doesn't take part? People will say that I've only won because Hammad was not there. They will never recognize me as the greatest poet of Kinda, even less so now that he has humiliated me two years in a row. I know everyone believes his victory was no accident, now that he has won a second time . . ."

He bit his lip, deep in thought.

"Will you hold the championship a third time, then?"

"Mmmm . . ." said Walid with a frown. "It's clear that I can't influence the judges' decision. How can I win? And what will I do if I lose again?"

"In my humble opinion, sire, if that should happen, you mustn't let him get away next time."

"What do you mean? Take him prisoner? How foolish can you be?"

"No, sire," the *rawi* answered with a cunning gleam in his eyes. "There are more subtle ways to keep a man in one place."

Walid turned toward him with interest.

"Speak, then. I'm listening."

✳   ✳   ✳

Everything returned to normal in Kinda in just a few days, but this time no one could easily forget the prince's humiliating defeat at the hands of Hammad ibn al-Haddad, the carpet weaver from al-Lakik. Many thought that Walid would never hold the competition again, but others were more levelheaded, claiming that the prince was a man of honor who would never feel satisfied until he showed his superiority to this peasant.

In time the latter were proven right. The news of another poetry competition went forth without delay, but with one important difference: This time the prize would be not only a bag of gold, but the post of royal historian for the palace of Kinda.

"How did this come about, Walid?" the king demanded as soon as his vizier told him the news. "What are you trying to do?"

Walid had expected such a question, and he was prepared for it.

"Father, the palace archive has been neglected for decades. The old man Ibrahim left it in a disgraceful condition."

"Old Ibrahim dedicated his whole life to that archive."

"And no one doubts his great work," the prince was quick to respond. "But he didn't have time to put all the documents in order, nor did he prepare anyone to take his place."

Ibrahim had been the archivist of Kinda for almost eighty years. His father had held the post before him, and his father's father before that. For generations, the Ibrahim family preserved within their prodigious memories all that they had witnessed over the course of their lives, and all that their elders or travelers from distant lands had told them. Only the last of the Ibrahims had decided to learn to read and write in order to record all the knowledge that had survived in him. Perhaps he didn't trust his memory as his ancestors had; perhaps he had guessed he would never have sons of his own. He spent several decades holed up in the palace, obsessively writing until death kept him from continuing. That had been before Walid was born, but King Hujr remembered the old archivist very well, and had mourned his loss.

No one had entered the archive since that time except for the young and curious prince, who had wanted to read his kingdom's history. But soon enough he had discovered that old Ibrahim's memories had been left in utter chaos and were all but useless. Walid had proposed to reorganize the archive himself, but the enormity of the task had overwhelmed him.

"They say that poetry is the *diwan* of the Arab peoples, our historical archive," Walid continued. "Who better then for the post of royal historian than Kinda's most excellent poet?"

King Hujr frowned as he considered his son's words.

"Do you take it for granted that once again you will not win the prize?" he asked.

"I *am* going to win," Walid answered in a dignified tone. "But in case I do not, I would like to be able to say that I was defeated by a man worthy of the post of royal historian, not by some unknown peasant."

He sensed approval in his father's face, and he knew he had won the argument.

Given that the king had not set foot in the archive since old Ibrahim's death, and that even if he had, he would have been unable to appreciate the state it was in, he had no idea that the prize being offered to the competition winner was a gift laced with venom.

No one else must have suspected, either, because once again the contest attracted a great number of participants. Becoming a functionary in the royal palace meant entering the elite of Kinda. It meant luxury and comfort for the rest of one's life, and the assurance that one's descendants would inherit the post, maintaining the family in Kinda's noble class as long as the dynasty of King Hujr ruled the land.

Few could resist such a prize, and so once again the plaza of Dhat Kahal was filled with people on the day of the competition.

Everything proceeded as usual. There were the same judges and almost the same contestants, with several newcomers joining in. This time, Hakim recited the prince's *qasida* directly after the performance of Amir, the carpet weaver's *rawi* and son, and both of them took the stage at midmorning, when half the *rawis* had given their recitations and another half remained. Set beside each other, the two *qasidas* were of an undeniable beauty and perfection.

But Hammad's *qasida* once again contained a certain something that Prince Walid's poem lacked.

Even so, the prince remained hopeful. The year before,

al-Nabiga had assured him that the judges would overlook this strange defect called "lack of heart" in two out of three parts of the *qasida*.

Still, the judges' verdict fell once again in the carpet weaver's favor. And while the entire plaza was cheering for Hammad, and the winner made his way haltingly toward the stage, three things happened.

First, al-Nabiga approached the prince and whispered:

"I am sorry, your highness. I do not doubt that you love your father, but the words you used for singing his praises sounded as empty and hollow as any that some foreign-born flatterer might use. Remember my advice: Speak with your heart, and you will be a good poet. A great poet. Perhaps the very best."

Walid had no time to answer, because now the king called him to his side. When he approached, his father made just one curt remark:

"It's over now."

He meant that there would be no further contests, and that as long as he was king, Walid would never go to Ukaz.

Strangely enough, these words did not hurt Walid as they might have in the past. He had no thought of his old dreams; he was focused only on Hammad ibn al-Haddad. He didn't know when he had begun to hate the other poet so much, nor did it matter. But he made a decision in that moment that would mark him for life, and this was the third important thing that happened.

He decided that Hammad ibn al-Haddad would suffer unspeakably for daring to cross his path.

*   *   *

That afternoon, King Hujr and his firstborn son received the trembling Hammad ibn al-Haddad for a royal audience.

"Sire . . . majesty . . ." the carpet weaver began. "I . . . I cannot accept the post that you have offered me."

The king arched his brow.

"And yet, you have accepted the bag of gold."

"Yes . . . yes . . . I . . . have three sons, sire. They all have dreams for the future. The oldest wants to be a merchant, and the second a shepherd; the third is still young, but I want to assure him enough means to fulfill his dreams too."

"So that is what you have done with the gold?" the king asked.

"Neither my wife nor I want anything for ourselves," Hammad explained. "We are happy in al-Lakik. But we want our sons to learn other trades and see the world. . . . With the first bag of gold we bought a few camels so that our oldest son could go to Palmyra and earn his fortune;

with the second we acquired a herd of sheep for our second son. This third bag of gold will be for Amir, my youngest, so that he can do what he wishes when he comes of age."

"A laudable effort on your part," the king agreed. "And have you given your older sons any assurances of helping them further in the merchant's or herdsman's trade?"

Hammad did not appear to understand the question, although Walid knew very well what the king had in mind.

"Your majesty, I . . . I can't say," said the carpet weaver. "They have worked very hard since they were small, all three of them. But the money we've earned from the carpets was never enough to help them become independent. I consider it my duty as their father to give them their first opportunity in life, but the rest they will have to do for themselves. That is why I entered the competition."

"Laudable again," said the king. "But this is no reason to turn down the honor that has been offered to you."

Hammad looked at the king and realized that insisting on continuing his humble way of life could be taken as a grave offense. By presenting himself at the competition, Hammad had agreed to the conditions if he won, and he was bound to the king and his tribe for life. He decided to try a different approach.

"Your majesty, I . . . " he muttered, lowering his eyes. "I must confess that I do not know how to read or write."

"That is no problem for a poet as great as yourself," the king replied at once. "You will learn how to read and write immediately, and then you'll be able to begin working in the archives."

Hammad ibn al-Haddad did not dare oppose the king of Kinda.

✿   ✿   ✿

Everything was done diligently and quickly. Hammad, his wife, Layla, and his youngest son, the *rawi* Amir, came to live at Dhat Kahal in the palace of the kings of Kinda. None of them was accustomed to the splendor of the court and they were unable to feel comfortable there, even though they saw what a relief it was not to have to worry over their daily sustenance anymore — Layla most of all.

Hammad began taking classes to learn to read and write. This was rather difficult for him, considering his great ability at composing verse, and he attributed this to age: Although the old carpet weaver was not yet such an elderly man, his face was furrowed with the hundreds of troubles he had known.

One day, Walid passed him in the palace and could not help but detain him a moment.

"Hammad . . ."

"Y . . . your highness?"

The prince looked at him intently. It was no secret in Kinda that Hammad had robbed him of his dreams and his honor. Surely the new royal historian knew by now that Walid had reason to hate him, and indeed a shadow of fear crept into the carpet weaver's eyes whenever Walid came by, although the prince was always careful to appear friendly and courteous toward him.

"For some time now, Hammad," said the prince, "I have wanted to ask you what your secret is."

"My . . . secret?"

Walid leaned toward him with a smile.

"How does a man like you manage to win a poetry competition three times in a row? Tell me: Do you have . . . a heart?"

Hammad swallowed hard.

"I . . . with all respect, I don't understand . . ."

"Never mind," said the prince. "Sooner or later I will find out."

And he went off down the corridor, leaving Hammad trembling and alone.

4

THE HISTORIAN

Hammad learned to read and write fluently. One day his teacher sent word to the prince of his proficiency. Walid called for the new royal historian at once, and he, the vizier, and two servants led Hammad to the archive.

The old carpet weaver was astonished.

It was an enormous room with high ceilings, its walls lined with endless shelves containing thousands of scroll cases — thousands and thousands.

"Here," Walid said softly, "is kept not only the history of our kingdom, but the history of all Arabia and all the Orient, and a great portion of the history of the West. But all the information is mixed together, out of order. Your work is to read all these scrolls and place them in chronological order."

"All of them?"

Walid gave him a brief glance.

"If one man could write them all, why couldn't one man read them?"

The new historian was desolate.

"But I will never complete . . ."

"Dear Hammad, this is a lifetime job. The post of royal historian is yours until death, and it will pass down to your sons if they choose to accept it. You told me, I believe, that the youngest has not yet decided on his future?"

Hammad could not respond right away.

"I had hoped this was a task that could be finished in a few years," he confessed. "So that I could return to al-Lakik."

Walid shook his head in disapproval, and exchanged glances with his vizier, who feigned a look of dismay.

"You offend my generosity, Hammad," Walid said. "I offer you a position that will maintain you in the royal palace for the rest of your life, and this is how you repay me. Even so, if you wish — seeing that you appreciate so little what I have tried to do for you — as soon as you finish sorting and classifying all these documents, you may go."

Hammad lifted his head and gave the prince a penetrating look that frightened him.

"Do you mean this, your highness?"

Walid hesitated a moment, but then considered that there was no danger in agreeing with this poor dreamer. The offer had been only a cruel jest.

"Of course." Walid turned away. "Place all of this in order, and I will let you return to al-Lakik."

"But your father . . ."

"I will speak with him when the time comes. If it ever does."

"So, then, to return to my home, I need only place the archive in order?" Hammad insisted.

Walid had an idea. He stifled a laugh.

"And weave a carpet," he added.

"A . . . carpet?"

"A beautiful carpet such as you've made in al-Lakik. As a farewell gift in thanks for being allowed to go," Walid explained. "We can arrange this between ourselves. You place the archive in order and weave a carpet to my liking, and I'll let you return home. Agreed?"

Looking about, Hammad took a deep breath and nodded.

"I agree."

Walid smiled.

"Good luck, Hammad," he said.

Turning to go, he saw the vizier and the two servants standing by the door, and again felt uncertain. He had given his word to Hammad, and these three had heard him. There was no turning back.

But he drove these thoughts from his mind. It didn't matter what he had promised to Hammad if the man finished putting the archive in order. He would never finish it. . . .

He left the room, followed by his servants, leaving the historian alone with the hundreds of thousands of scrolls.

*　*　*

Hammad resigned himself to staying in the palace for the rest of his days, and tried to lead a normal life. Thus he spent the morning and part of the afternoon in the archive, familiarizing himself with its contents, and dedicated the rest of his time to being with his family and trying to adapt himself to courtly ways. Nevertheless, palace life oppressed him, and soon he found himself rising early to work more hours in the archive, holding on to the hope of one day completing his task.

His family was unhappy too. Layla was a simple woman who did not fit in with the rest of the courtiers, and Amir, a restless and curious boy, felt the walls of the palace holding him back, imprisoning his spirit, keeping him from enjoying the immensity of the desert, even though it was not forbidden for him to leave.

Hammad realized all of this soon enough.

"Go back to the oasis," he said to them one day. "When I finish my work, I will come home to you."

"We won't abandon you," Layla replied. "How could we live so long without you, Hammad?"

"We should all escape," said Amir.

But Hammad shook his head.

"Doing that would be a grave offense to the king and his son. They would hunt us down and kill us."

"I mean we should escape far away from Kinda," the boy insisted.

Hammad hesitated a moment.

"It can't be, my son," he said. "I don't want to place you in danger. Go. I will be all right."

Layla came closer and looked into his eyes.

"The prince wants only to destroy you, Hammad. I have seen it in his face."

"I know, Layla. That is why I must stay. If I work in the archive morning, noon, and night, I will finish sooner than he thinks, and then he will let me go."

"How do you know he will?"

"Because I have made him promise. Walid is a prince, and a prince who doesn't live up to his word is nothing. He knows that. Layla, go back to al-Lakik, I beg you. You will be safe there."

Layla lowered her head and said no more.

*   *   *

Hammad bade his family farewell at the palace door. He watched them walk down the street, turning often to repeat their good-byes or exchange another farewell glance.

[43]

He looked and waved back without moving from his spot until they were completely out of sight. He knew he would have this image of them in his heart for the rest of his life.

Slowly he turned, reentered the palace, closed himself up in the archive, and hardly left it again. He called for food and drink to be brought to him at certain hours of the day, and he hauled a cot to the edge of the room. He found a small toilet in a corner that old Ibrahim must have built. And he decided that with these he had all he needed. He began to read.

Days, weeks, and months passed. At first it was difficult and he made slow progress, but with time he became a more fluent reader and grew accustomed to the cramped calligraphy of the old archivist who had spilled out his entire memory on the scrolls.

As he read, he made categories. He decided to make the first category geography, and separated the documents into empires, kingdoms, principalities, tribes, and clans. Next, he had to reread everything to arrange the scrolls of each classification in chronological order, according to which monarch ruled at the time and place that the manuscript described.

He learned a great deal. He had traveled during his youth, but the knowledge of history, told in old Ibrahim's precise and impeccable style, opened his mind in an extraordinary way. He understood that the world was much larger than he had ever dreamed — that he was only one small link in the great chain of humankind, whose origins were hidden in the mists of time. And this made him feel both humble and powerful: humble, for being little more than a grain of sand in an immense desert; powerful, because he was a part of something great, and because this history was also his own.

For his part, Prince Walid hardly knew what to make of the dedication of this man he had vowed to destroy.

"You were right about him, my son," said King Hujr whenever Walid reminded him of the historian. "Busy all day long in there, like old Ibrahim. He is a worthy replacement, no doubt about it."

Sometimes Walid visited the archive, and he was always impressed by what he saw. Hammad had emptied the shelves, and their contents lay spread on the floor in jumbled heaps — hundreds of thousands of scrolls enclosed in cases that seemed on the verge of bursting. The royal historian would pick up a document, read through it rapidly, and sort it into a new, much more orderly pile. Sometimes he would stop to consult an old map he had hung on the wall, or to collect one of the piles on a certain shelf.

"Here is the history of Greece," he would say to the prince. "And up here I am going to place the history of Persia. Over there . . ."

Walid would interrupt him gently and always managed to change the topic.

"Travels through the desert? Oh, yes," said Hammad without pausing in his work. "When I was a young man I traveled from al-Hira to Yathrib, and some time later, I came with my family to Kinda. I liked the experience very much."

Or:

"Yes, I truly owe a great deal to your noble father, sir. He allowed me and my family to establish ourselves in his kingdom. For humble people like us it is important to find a place that is governed by someone wise and just, where we can live in peace."

Or:

"My teacher was not a great poet, sir. But I needed work and my parents, you understand, were very poor. So I worked with him for a while as his *rawi* — less than a year, I believe. That was when I learned the form of the *qasida*, although I didn't know how to make poetry until much later on. . . ."

Walid would keep on interrogating him in subtle fashion, but the historian was a man of few words, something that surprised the prince very much — he had expected more from such a poet. Nothing that he said explained why his verses contained "heart."

One day the prince asked him about the woman he had portrayed in the *nasib* of his *qasidas*, adding, "She must be a very beautiful woman."

Hammad turned to look at him in surprise.

"But sire, you know her. She is my wife, Layla."

Walid let out a little laugh. Layla was neither young nor beautiful. The prince even found her rather vulgar — hardly capable of inspiring poetry from anyone, even less so the lovely verses Hammad had created.

"Don't make fun of me; surely you are recalling some passionate young love."

"No, sire, not I . . ."

"Or else you are as blind as my father."

Retreating into an offended silence, the historian turned back to the mountain of documents. Nor did the prince speak. They remained quiet until Hammad declared tenderly:

"I love her. The woman I see when I look at her is the woman of my poems: I see her not with the eyes of my face but with the eyes of the heart."

Walid nearly gave a start. That word again: *heart*. . . .

He pondered for a long time what Hammad had said, but he could not understand it, which made his hatred grow all the more. But he wouldn't kill him; no, not yet. He wanted to learn his real secret, the one that gave his verses their special magic. And what's more, he knew that keeping Hammad in that archive was itself a death sentence. If the old carpet weaver persisted, it was only because the hope of returning to his family one day sustained him. . . .

Nearly four years passed, during which time only a few things changed. There were more scroll cases on the shelves than on the floor of the archive, but Hammad kept working morning, noon, and night. Walid remained devoted to his princely duties; at the age of twenty-three, he was still a handsome young man. His literary circle was active, and whenever anyone would ask about the great poet who had beaten him three times, Walid would shrug and say:

"He must prefer the job of historian to that of poet, since he spends every day holed up in the archive. I doubt he will be writing poems again."

Walid's own verses continued to circulate throughout the land of Kinda, thanks to Hakim, who still served him dutifully. After a while, people forgave the prince his losses in the poetry contest, saying that Walid had been so young then, and now that he was grown, he must surely have made progress in his art. Now and then, someone would recall a stray verse from one of Hammad's three *qasidas,* but no one doubted anymore that Walid was the greatest poet that Kinda had ever known.

Nor was there the slightest doubt that for some time now, it was Walid who truly governed the kingdom's affairs. King Hujr had fallen very ill, and for months had been unable to leave his bed. At first Walid had replaced him only occasionally, when the king was too indisposed to receive some visitor. But over time it had become habitual to see the prince presiding over the audience chambers, until at last the king no longer appeared there at all.

Walid was not yet the official sovereign of Kinda, and he often went to consult with his father on important matters. But more and more, the king's responses became confused and incoherent.

It was no secret to the people of Kinda that their king was dying. Years before, the thought of being ruled by the noble Prince Walid would have pleased any of his subjects. But now, many were not so sure.

Walid had changed. On the outside, the change was only slight and subtle, hard to define, but it implied a great transformation within. He remained courteous, generous, and brave, but in his eyes there was a bitter look; his smile bore a trace of irony, and in his words one heard a certain harshness of tone. He no longer laughed as often as before; his thin smile seemed cunning and calculating. No one could tell what went on in his head, except perhaps for his faithful shadow, Hakim. The rumor was that when the king died, the vizier would be overthrown and Hakim would take his post.

This was the prince before whom, one day, a pale and hollow-eyed skeleton of a man presented himself. It took Walid a moment to recognize him.

"I have finished, your majesty," Hammad announced.

5

THE ENLIGHTENED ONE

A pair of guards was already approaching, but the prince motioned them back and observed the historian carefully.

Hammad had grown alarmingly thin, and his erratic and unkempt gray beard reached to his chest. His face was terribly pale. His eyes blinked rapidly, as if pained by the light of the audience room, accustomed as they were to permanent shadow. A strange and feeble light shone in them.

But even though his outward appearance was that of a longtime prisoner, something in his look announced with a great cry that he was a free man.

Walid did not like this.

"What did you say?" he asked.

"That I have finished placing the archive in order. I have fulfilled my part of the agreement, and now you must fulfill yours."

"How dare you speak to me this way?" the prince burst out in anger. "You don't even have the decency to present yourself before me in the proper manner!"

Hammad said nothing, maintaining his steady and defiant look. He bore no resemblance at all to the man who, six years before, had won the first poetry competition of Kinda and had come forward blushing, stuttering, tripping over himself, to collect the prize.

Walid understood that if what the historian said were true, he would have no reason to keep him in the palace, because he could not go back on his word. But it was impossible for Hammad to have completed the work so soon. Four years . . . surely the man must be trying to deceive him.

"I will have to come see for myself," he said, in a somewhat calmer tone.

Hammad nodded.

"Whenever you like."

Walid's steady manner wavered before the historian's determination, and a trace of fear appeared for a moment in his eyes — but he recovered at once.

"First, you must bathe and dress and groom yourself properly."

Once more, Hammad agreed.

✻   ✻   ✻

An hour later, the prince of Kinda walked toward the archive, followed by Hakim.

"He could not have finished already, sire," said the *rawi*. "It's impossible."

Walid frowned. "Working so many hours, and at such a pace? It could be. Damn it all, I gave him my word."

Hakim coughed hoarsely.

"With all due respect, sire, the situation has changed a great deal since then. If you made this carpet weaver disappear, your father would probably never find out."

Walid shook his head.

"No, Hakim, the people still remember him."

"But it's been nearly four years since he won the . . ."

"I know! But everyone knows that he is still alive, and if he died, they would know that as well. The rabble always finds out about these things somehow."

Hakim tried to argue, but the prince silenced him with a gesture and went on:

"What's more, Hakim, the truth is that I don't want him to die. I want him to live for years and years, the longer the better, so that he can suffer as much as possible. . . ."

He stopped at the entrance to the archive, so suddenly that the *rawi* almost tripped over him.

"And I have yet to find out the secret of his art," he added in a low voice.

"There are ways of torturing him," the *rawi* hastened to point out.

"I have the feeling that even under torture he wouldn't tell me," sighed the prince, opening the chamber doors, "because I fear he doesn't know."

They entered and looked around, confirming Walid's worst fears: The scroll cases were perfectly arranged on properly labeled shelves, with not a single scroll out of place. To make sure, the prince took down one of the scroll cases, opened it, and examined its contents: The documents had to do with Egypt in the time of Ramses III. He replaced it on the shelf and took down the next: It contained scrolls concerning Egypt in the time of Ramses IV.

Suppressing a powerful wave of anger mixed with panic, Walid continued to peruse the archive. He saw that its largest section was dedicated to the history of Arabia, and he searched for the part that contained documents about his own kingdom. This too was of a considerable size. To his surprise, he found a scroll case full of documents on his father's reign, going practically up to that very year. The calligraphy was not that of old Ibrahim.

"I have taken the liberty of bringing the archive a bit more up to date," Hammad said hoarsely from the doorway. "I hope his highness finds this to his liking."

Walid and his *rawi* turned around. Hammad seemed

much more at ease now, but still bore that strange light in his eyes.

"Tell me," gasped the prince. "How did you obtain this information?"

The historian shrugged.

"When one lives in an oasis, one often hears news come in with the merchant caravans," he said.

Walid didn't know what to say.

"An excellent job," he stammered.

"Thank you, sire."

"How have you managed it?"

Hammad smiled bitterly.

"With hard work, tenacity, and determination, sire, one can accomplish anything in the world. That is how all great things are done."

"I see," Walid muttered. He opened his mouth to say more, but stopped short.

"I suppose, then," said Hammad, "that I have your permission to weave the carpet I promised you, and to return home as soon as I have finished it, do I not?"

"Carpet?" repeated Walid.

"A carpet made to order," the historian reminded him. "Tell me, what kind of carpet do you wish?"

The prince remembered the conditions he had imposed almost four years before: In exchange for his freedom, Hammad must organize the archive and weave a carpet. Walid had said it in jest, believing that his rival would never weave such a carpet, because he would never finish placing the archive in order. And now only this carpet stood between Hammad and his family.

A cunning smile spread across the prince of Kinda's face.

"Made to order, eh?" he murmured.

He looked about for inspiration. All he saw were cases of scrolls on shelves that reached to the ceiling: tons and tons of history.

A thought came to him, and indicating the entire archive with a wave of his hand, he demanded:

"I would like a carpet that encompasses all of this."

Hakim looked at him in confusion, and Hammad lost all composure at once.

"Wh . . . what did you say?" he stuttered. "I don't believe I heard you properly."

"You heard me perfectly well," Walid replied coldly. "I want a carpet that contains the entire history of the human race. Who better to make it than you, a weaver who has read everything contained in this room?"

"B . . . but all of that could never fit onto one carpet. . . ."

The prince placed a hand condescendingly on the archivist's shoulder.

"My dear Hammad, you are a great poet," he said, "and everyone knows that the art of poetry is founded on conciseness. You won the competition because you captured all the beauty of the world in just a few verses. So I am convinced that it would not be difficult for you to condense all of history onto one carpet. I will supply you with anything you need."

Hammad said nothing as the full weight of the prince's impossible request came over him. Suddenly, his legs could no longer hold him up, and he fell to his knees before Walid ibn Hujr.

"Sire," he said hoarsely. "I cannot do it."

"Come, come, Hammad. I have given you a post that many others would kill for. You won't deny me one simple carpet, will you?"

"Sire," Hammad sighed. "I beg you. . . ."

But Walid only laughed, and Hakim joined in. The prince turned his back on the carpet weaver and walked away, leaving the archive without a backward glance, followed by his faithful *rawi*. And in the middle of the room they left a man crushed by despair.

For several days Hammad could be seen wandering aimlessly through the palace. He had a faraway look in his eyes and mumbled incoherent phrases, and many people thought he had lost his senses. One day, in a fit of murderous rage, he tried to attack the prince in the garden and had to be subdued by the guards, who beat him unconscious. Then they carried him off to his room, on Walid's express orders, and let him sleep.

Hammad slept for seven days and nights, and on the seventh night he woke.

His first thought was that all of this had been a dream, that he had never entered the poetry competition and had never met Prince Walid ibn Hujr. But right away he knew that the bed he was lying on was too soft to be his own.

In a moment he was seated at the window, contemplating the beauty of the heavens dotted with stars, the desert far beyond the city and its seven towers, the moon's mysterious glow. The image of Layla burned in his heart. He missed her and their three sons so much.

He knew that he would never see them again.

But Hammad had no thought of giving up. He leaped up, threw a cape over himself, and left the chamber. He would escape. He would reach al-Lakik, gather up his wife and youngest son, and together they would flee someplace where Walid's cold hand could never reach them.

With an almost suicidal determination, overcome with despair, he passed through the darkened corridors of the palace toward the servants' gate. Reaching the gate and even crossing the garden were no problem, but getting past the main gate of the palace would not be so simple. In truth, Hammad was not a prisoner at all; he could come and go about the city as he chose. But Walid knew all of his movements, and if he suspected that the old historian had abandoned his post, he would have him tracked down.

Hammad sighed almost imperceptibly, covered his head and face with the hood, and slipped through the garden. He had to try. He approached the guards and saluted them in the ordinary way. Neither of them made the slightest response. Hammad relaxed a little. It had been so long since he had crossed this gate that the guards had forgotten his face, and took him for some servant or other. Still, he didn't have much time. At dawn, Walid would realize he was missing and send his guards after him. Until then, he was free.

* * *

A few minutes passed before one of the guards, having thought it over carefully, commented to the other:

"Say, wasn't that the madman who tried to attack the prince?"

"Could be," said the other after a moment. "Servants all look alike."

"Should we have let him go?"

"Why not? His highness didn't order us to stop him. Besides, if he's dangerous, it's better for him to be gone, isn't it?"

But the first guard was troubled.

"Maybe we should send word."

"To the prince? And wake him up? You're mad. If it bothers you so much, we'll inform him at dawn. If you're right and he's really escaped, we'll go after him. You know he won't get very far."

This reasoning didn't ease the first guard's conscience.

"I'd better go after him," he declared.

He fastened his sword to his belt and disappeared into the dark and narrow streets of Dhat Kahal.

* * *

Hammad sensed that he was being pursued. His heart beating furiously, he hid around a corner and held his breath as the guard passed by.

But then a snorting sound gave him a start and drew the guard's attention. Hammad realized that he had hidden next to a stable, and the horses, grown restless from his presence, were about to betray him.

He saw the guard approaching and knew that there was only one way out. He entered the stable and leaped onto one of the horses.

The animal rose up on its hind legs and neighed hysterically. Not knowing how to ride, Hammad was frozen with terror, but he held onto the horse's mane with all his might. Just then the guard opened the stable door, and that was all the horse needed to fly out of there at full gallop. The guard got out of the horse's path at the last moment and stood there powerless, watching the old carpet weaver escape, bucking like a loose bale of hay on the back of the stolen horse.

Hammad reached the edge of Dhat Kahal and tore into the desert. Anyone else would have known what madness it was to attempt such a journey without provisions, but Hammad had only one thought in his head: fleeing, getting as far away as he could from Walid and his impossible demands.

The horse galloped onward, out of control. Hammad tried to situate himself better on its back, but he lost his balance, slipped, and fell to the ground before he knew it. . . .

He slammed against the cold sand and dizzily raised his head. The horse that had brought him this far was now a speck disappearing in the night.

Hammad sighed. He was alone in the desert without food, water, or a horse. But he could not go back, because Walid's people were coming after him. There was only one possibility: to go on ahead until he could go no farther.

He crossed the depths of night, climbing up and down dunes lit softly by moonlight, disregarding cold and weariness. Layla's face seemed to smile on him from the night sky, urging him on. *I'm coming, Layla*, thought Hammad. *I'm coming, Amir. Soon I will be with you.* . . .

But even though he put all his strength into it, he did not get very far, just as the guard had predicted. When he tried to run faster he tripped, rolled down a dune, and remained motionless against the cold, hard sand. For the first time he realized that all thought of escape had been senseless, and that he would never reach al-Lakik alone and on foot. He looked up at the starry sky and wept, and the desert swallowed his tears.

✳   ✳   ✳

Walid was awakened by his worried vizier at an unreasonably early hour. As he dressed in a hurry, he told himself he would dismiss the man as soon as he became king.

"What's going on?" he asked as soon as he emerged into the hall.

"Sire, it's the historian. The guards tell me that he has escaped. . . ."

Walid jumped as though someone had pinched him.

"And what are you waiting for? Why haven't you sent the guards after him?"

"That isn't necessary, sire, because he returned just an hour ago. He's . . . I don't know . . . half crazy. He took over a room next to the harem that the women use for spinning and weaving, turned everything upside down, and set up an enormous loom. Next he started demanding all kinds of wool and dye. He said that you promised to supply him with anything he needed."

"Anything he needed for what?"

"To weave a carpet, sire."

It all seemed like madness to Walid, but he ran to see for himself what was going on.

He found Hammad in the midst of a great commotion, sitting on the floor with his legs crossed, surrounded by mountains of carded and spun wool of every color, separating one skein from another and ceaselessly giving orders to a few confused and sleepy-eyed servants who kept bringing him more and more woolen thread.

"What are you doing?" asked the prince in astonishment.

"I am making a carpet," Hammad calmly replied. "A carpet that will contain the entire history of the human race."

"But that's impossible!" exclaimed the vizier.

Hammad raised his head toward him.

"It's not impossible," he said. "Nothing is impossible."

Walid and his vizier took several steps back, terrified by the look on Hammad's face: His eyes were aglow with a strange, almost inhuman light.

"He's lost his senses," muttered the frightened vizier.

Walid said nothing, but he turned his back on the weaver and left, and the vizier followed him.

"Give him anything he asks for," Walid ordered.

"But sire . . . !"

"I promised him all the materials he needed for

weaving a beautiful carpet, and a prince never goes back on his word."

"But he's crazy!"

"Even so, I am sure he will weave me a beautiful carpet, even if it's not the kind he is promising to make," he answered with a smile. "As you say, he's a poor madman. So let's leave him alone to do his weaving. Locked up there, he can't do anyone much harm."

The vizier was not so sure, but said nothing more.

Walid spent the rest of the day tortured by doubt. He sensed that Hammad was dangerous, that he ought to kill him. But the carpet weaver's eyes had spoken to him of something so boundless that the prince was afraid of awakening its anger.

Walid was a poet. He could see what the vizier hadn't yet — that Hammad ibn al-Haddad was no longer entirely human.

6

THE KING

In the days that followed, confusion ruled over the palace. Soon everyone had heard the rumors about a madman who wanted to weave a carpet, but the most surprising part was this: Not only was the prince not trying to stop him, but he had given orders to help him in whatever way necessary. The madman asked for more and more skeins of wool of every imaginable color, and when it was no longer possible to supply them in the fineness and tones he demanded, he called for raw wool and set up all the tools he needed to card and spin and dye it himself. No one knew how he managed to carry out this entire process himself, nor how he achieved shades of color never before seen just by mixing everyday dyes together. When he felt that he had all the necessary materials, Hammad dismantled the wool preparation workshop and sat down before the loom with all the skeins of wool around him, those that had been brought in from outside and those that he had prepared himself.

And he began to weave, and never stopped. Those who had the chance to watch him swore that they had never seen a weaver like him, one who used wools of so many different colors at once and apparently never made the slightest mistake. His fingers glided rapidly over the loom without a trace of hesitation.

Soon it was well known that the man never slept and practically never ate, always weaving tirelessly away, and that if he kept on at this pace he would no doubt die of exhaustion before long. Once the prince tried to get him to eat and rest, but it was no use, and the man was simply left to work in peace.

Yet Walid found the rumors about him more and more disturbing. According to Hakim, the people knew that this madman was the historian who had once been a great poet. As the months went by and Hammad did not collapse, they began to say that the carpet weaver was inspired by a *djinn*.

Like any man of the desert, Walid knew what this meant. According to popular legend, great men, great poets, and great artists were enlightened by the primal forces of the desert. Walid had grown used to hearing such praise about himself and the *djinns* from admirers and flatterers ever since he was a boy. In fact, he had come to believe it — had come to think that those powerful lords of the desert favored him because he deserved it. And now his subjects were saying the same thing about this carpet weaver: that he was inspired by *djinns*.

But that alone is not what bothered Walid; rather, it was that this time, people said such things seriously, pronouncing the name of Hammad and his invisible helpers with reverence, respect, and fear.

Still, the prince did nothing to stifle the rumors, perhaps because he himself feared they were true. Strange ideas began to form in his mind and take shape during his sleepless nights. *Djinns* . . . of course, why hadn't he thought of it before? How otherwise could an illiterate peasant win a poetry competition three consecutive times, organize the archive in only four years, and attempt to weave a carpet containing the entire history of the human race?

"But that is impossible, sire," said Hakim. "Why would the *djinns* take notice of someone like him?"

"And what if they have, Hakim?" The prince trembled in terror. "And what if we have angered the *djinns* by conspiring against their chosen one?"

"If it worries you so much, tell him to stop weaving the carpet."

"I have done so already, but he does not want to stop. I promised him his freedom but he answered me that it was too late now. Too late — why? Do you understand, Hakim?"

The *rawi* nodded.

"What I understand is that the poor devil has lost his mind, sire. If he disturbs you so much, you should get rid of him. There are poisons capable of killing a person without leaving the slightest trace. No one would know that he had been assassinated."

"And if he isn't mad? I don't want to take the risk. I've seen something in his eyes, something supernatural that no man ought to challenge."

Hakim shrugged and made no answer, but the gesture showed clearly that he did not agree with this interpretation. Walid pursed his lips in uncertainty.

"Wait until he finishes the carpet," his helper suggested. "Then we will see whether he has been inspired by *djinns*."

Time passed in Kinda — in its villages, in its capital, in its small patch of desert, and in the palace of King Hujr.

People stopped bringing supplies into Hammad's chamber because he had everything he needed. They stopped bringing him food because he no longer ate. They even moved the harem to another part of the palace, because the proximity of this weaving madman made the women uneasy. The rumors died down in time, and Hammad ibn al-Haddad faded gradually into oblivion.

Even Prince Walid stopped worrying about him. Hammad went on weaving and weaving but never finished the carpet, and so the idea that he was enlightened by *djinns* lost its power. The prince decided that, just as his *rawi* had said, the carpet weaver was nothing but an ordinary madman.

Besides, Walid was busier than ever now that he had taken over the reins of the kingdom. What everyone feared was coming to pass: King Hujr was dying.

He passed three days in a delirium with terrible pain and fever. Walid spent as much time as he could at the old king's side, listening to his ravings. They were alone when his father signaled him to come near.

"Yes, Father?"

"Listen to me, son, because I don't have much time left. You will inherit the kingdom, and you know what this means, because I have taught you."

The old man paused, gasping for breath. Walid tried to keep him from speaking, but the king continued:

"Even so, I am going to give you something now that is worth more than a kingdom. It is a piece of advice that I want you to keep in mind your whole life, because it will be useful to you."

"I'm listening, Father."

"Listen well: We are all responsible for our actions, both for good and for evil. And life always returns to you what you give it. Never forget this, son. Never forget that life makes us pay a price. . . ."

Walid did not understand, but he nodded his head.

The king turned his head toward him and looked at him as though he could see.

"Remember my words, Walid."

The prince did not know what to say. He was going to ask whether his father felt better, but the king's body suffered another convulsion and his mind returned to its feverish wanderings. Soon after, King Hujr died.

All that happened next was very confusing for Walid — the funeral rites, his family's grief, the condolences expressed by representatives of every tribe and village, the weeping, the ceremony of taking possession of the kingdom.

Walid ibn Hujr was the new king of Kinda, but even though he had been anticipating his father's death and acting in his name for quite some time, he still felt mystified and confused. Years before, Walid had decided that when he became the king of Kinda he would go to Ukaz and win the poetry competition. Next he would extend his kingdom by conquering a few small neighboring states. He would make Dhat Kahal such a flourishing city that all the merchants would stop their caravans there, and in time, he would surpass the rulers of Palmyra, Alexandria, and Samarkand in wealth and power.

But none of this made sense to him now. Amid the long succession of funeral visits from tribal sheiks and ambassadors from other kingdoms, Walid could think of nothing but his father's last words, which had reminded him for some reason that deep inside his palace, a man was tirelessly weaving a carpet.

The night of his coronation, after everything was quiet again, King Walid went to visit Hammad ibn al-Haddad.

He entered the chamber cautiously and looked around. The stray materials were piled up in complete disorder. Hammad was weaving his carpet in a corner of the room by the trembling light of a single oil lamp.

In other circumstances, Walid would not have entered alone. He still remembered that Hammad had once tried to attack him. But that night, Walid's first night as king of Kinda, none of that was important. He and the carpet weaver were once again in each other's presence.

Walid stepped closer to see Hammad more clearly. He was seated on the floor with his legs crossed and his back hunched, leaning so close over the loom that his nose nearly brushed against it.

Walid took another step forward, intending to observe how the weaver worked, but the man noticed his presence, stood up at once, and turned toward him suspiciously, hiding the unfinished carpet behind his back.

"Who are you and what do you want?" he asked in a hoarse voice.

Walid noticed that Hammad's eyes blinked more than

normal, straining to see in the darkness, and he realized that the man had been working night and day for so long, first in the archive and now with the carpet, that he had ruined his eyesight.

He kept silent a moment, observing the man who had been the greatest poet of Kinda and who was now not even a shadow of the Hammad of that time. Pale, skeletal, with his hair and beard grown wild, Hammad ibn al-Haddad was a ravaged and beaten man who would surely never succeed in creating the carpet he had promised Walid.

The king felt a dark and savage sensation of delight. He had done it. He had broken the carpet weaver's spirit. But such a victory was ice-cold to him. Without knowing why, he felt deep inside that this was not what he wanted, even though he had desired it for such a long time.

"Who are you, intruder?" Hammad repeated. "Speak!"

Walid paused a moment before answering. When he did, his tone was serene, calm, and cool.

"I am the king."

Just when Walid supposed that he had not recognized his voice, the carpet weaver replied:

"So your father has died at last, and you are the new king of Kinda."

"So it is."

"And now you can kill me if you wish."

"That is correct."

A silence fell between them. Then the king asked:

"And what are you weaving, if I may ask?"

"You already know, sire: a carpet containing the entire history of the human race."

"You are mad, Hammad."

"All great poets are mad, sire. It is the madness of the *djinns.*"

Walid could not keep from trembling.

"Let me see it."

But the weaver hid his work even more firmly behind him.

"It's not finished."

"That doesn't matter."

"It does to me. It is not just any carpet, O king of Kinda. Nor is it merely an extraordinary carpet. It is much more than that."

"What is it, then?"

"A treasure-house of humanity. It cannot be touched by unworthy hands, or looked at by ignorant eyes."

Walid stretched forward as though pulled by a spring.

"How dare you? You consider me unworthy and ignorant? And who do you think you are, miserable peasant?"

"Someone wiser than you, sire."

Shaking with rage, the king threw himself at Hammad to push him aside and see that precious unfinished carpet of his. But the weaver stood still as a stone before him, staring at the king in fury.

Walid stopped suddenly, trembling. There was something so powerful and disturbing in that look that he felt like a miserable insect in the immensity of the desert.

"Go away and let me work," said Hammad. "Know that you are a mere mortal who has unleashed powers more terrible than a mighty storm, and that as a mortal, you cannot stop their wrath. Not anymore. It is far too late."

Walid said nothing, and turned and left the room. He looked back only once before he closed the door, and he saw Hammad leaning over his carpet again, small and hunchbacked and insignificant.

Walid ibn Hujr did not turn out to be the kind of king everyone had hoped he would be. At first he made an effort to continue his princely customs, but he seemed absentminded in diplomatic meetings and distracted in expeditions through the desert. Even his literary circle no longer interested him, so that most of the poets soon abandoned the court of Kinda and sought shelter under the wings of more generous rulers.

Walid kept by his side only his old *rawi* Hakim, who no longer functioned as such, since his patron had not composed any verses for quite some time. Hakim's position in the palace was no longer clear, because the long-desired post of royal vizier had not come his way.

Walid contented himself with leaving things as they were before his father's death.

The new king of Kinda had gone from being a courtly, generous, open-minded, and friendly prince to a pale, brooding, preoccupied, and often distant man. Wagging tongues swore that some beautiful woman dominated his thoughts and prevented him from sleeping, but no one had been able to find out who she was. Not even Hakim knew the real cause of his distress. He too had forgotten the madman who was weaving an impossible carpet in a corner of the palace.

But Walid could not forget, even though he seldom summoned enough courage to visit Hammad in his workshop. When he did so, always at night and always alone, he restricted himself to watching from the doorway. If he came nearer, Hammad would hide his work behind his back and refuse to show it. The supernatural aura that surrounded the weaver commanded such respect from the king of Kinda that he never dared to defy him. If Hammad had asked to go home, Walid would not have held him back — not anymore.

But Hammad never asked.

One night, when the king entered the chamber, he found it in darkness, lit only by a trace of starlight filtering through the window. For a moment he thought that Hammad had fled at last, but then he heard the sound of fingers passing wool through the loom, and made out the shape of a starved and hunchbacked body leaning over the carpet as always.

"Hammad, you are weaving in the dark."

"That is possible, sire. I had not noticed."

Puzzled, Walid left to find a lamp. When he returned, bringing a light into the room, the weaver did not even look up. The king of Kinda was amazed to see what had happened.

Hammad had gone completely blind. And yet he went on weaving.

✻   ✻   ✻

After that, the king spaced his visits much further apart. Something like remorse over the great atrocity he had committed began to gnaw at his heart. Having abandoned poetry some time ago, he began to wonder whether it had ever been important to him after all, or worth the trouble of holding three competitions and destroying a man's life. He remembered with frightening clarity his father's last words before dying: "We are all responsible for our actions. . . . Life makes us pay a price. . . ."

Hakim noticed his master's strangeness, how he fled all company and became more and more silent. The king began to leave many matters in the old vizier's hands.

Something was happening to the soul of Walid ibn Hujr, and his people could not explain what it was or why he acted this way.

One night, after several sleepless hours, Walid decided that he could stand it no longer. "I will beg and plead with him to go," he said to himself. "I will offer him everything I own, despite all the shame it will bring on me, because I don't want him here anymore. I want him to go back to his oasis and his family; I want him to leave me in peace and take that carpet far away. If he doesn't leave of his own accord, I will send him away by force."

And having made this resolution, the king rose from his bed, took up a lamp, and went to Hammad's workshop.

"Listen to me, weaver," he began. "I have decided . . ."

But he stopped suddenly, not finding at all what he had expected.

For once, Hammad ibn al-Haddad was not bent over the loom, weaving his carpet. He was lying on the floor, and he was dead.

Walid did not dare move at first. Then he slowly came closer to make sure of what he already knew: Hammad had died of exhaustion at last. His body was extraordinarily thin — so fragile and slight that it hardly seemed possible he could have survived for so long in such a condition. Even so, his face bore a peaceful expression, a gentle, satisfied smile. Next to him, Walid saw, was a carpet, large enough to wrap a grown man's body inside it.

At a glance it seemed like just an ordinary carpet, beautiful and elaborate but no different from other beautiful carpets that Walid had seen in his life, and he had seen many. The king felt disappointed and relieved at once: In the end, it had turned out that Hammad ibn al-Haddad was nothing but a poor madman.

He picked up the carpet to study it more carefully. The design was intricate, laborious, and hard to make out. Walid raised the lamp and fixed his gaze on it.

There was something hypnotizing . . . dizzying . . . in that pattern. Walid blinked a couple of times and looked again. . . . Then he let out a cry of fright. The lines were moving! The labyrinthine design undulated as if it had a life of its own. Suddenly it began to spin and spin, and chaotic images formed in the king of Kinda's mind, moving and shifting and twirling around, showing him landscapes and faces and impossible shapes, people who moved too fast to be seen and spoke too fast to be understood.

Walid cried out in a desperate effort to escape from the carpet's sorcery. He threw the lamp far from him and covered his eyes to keep from seeing any more. In absolute horror, he turned and fled, leaving behind the weaver's body and the wondrous, monstrous carpet he had created.

7

THE THIEF

The king of Kinda stayed alone in his chamber for several hours, trembling, not daring to leave, his mind a swarm of chaotic thoughts. When he could begin to set aside the disturbing images he had seen in the carpet, he thought of Hammad.

He had done it . . . the old devil had done it! And the implications of this filled him with terror. A lowly carpet weaver had created something impossible, supernatural, almost divine. A miracle.

Now that Hammad was gone, all kinds of memories flooded the king's mind. The carpet weaver's beautiful *qasidas*, his tireless work in the archive, his tiny body hunched over the loom where he had accomplished his great last work — a fantastical thing made real — a carpet containing the entire history of the human race.

Hammad might have been the greatest artist that Arabia, and perhaps the whole world, had ever known.

And he, Walid ibn Hujr, had put him to death. Out of pure envy, he had destroyed a body that contained a great soul, because his own spirit had never deserved to be compared with that of the amazing weaver of carpets.

"What have I done?" the king of Kinda groaned. "O *djinns*, what have I done?"

When the night sky began to brighten at the horizon, Walid got up and left his chamber. He ran to the room where the body of the weaver and his impossible carpet lay. He rolled the body in a thick cloth and dragged it through the corridors to one of the side doors of the palace. There he ordered a servant, a dim-witted fellow who never asked questions, to carry it on horseback to the oasis of al-Lakik.

Once this was done, he returned to the workshop and rolled up the carpet without daring to look at it. He dragged it to a safe room nearby where he kept his treasure, closed the door, drew a thick chain across it, and fastened it with an enormous lock. Then he placed the key under his shirt on a golden chain that he always wore around his neck and swore to himself that he would never enter that room again.

*   *   *

Many things changed after that. Walid withdrew even further inside himself. He became a shy and solitary man, tormented by guilt and regret. The splendor of his court, which had declined a great deal since the time of King Hujr, faded completely. Walid was no longer a gracious host or a generous ruler.

At first he maintained his position among his troops, leading suicidal missions and expeditions, fighting recklessly against the enemies of the kingdom as if seeking his own death. But when he did not manage to die an honorable death, he grew tired of dancing on the edge of a sword blade, and once again he withdrew into the palace and his gloomy silence.

Little by little the vizier took over the reins of government, and he managed to keep the kingdom on course a few months more. But soon the word began to spread that King Walid was ill, in body, or mind, or perhaps both. According to rumors, he had renounced all pleasure, ate little and slept even less, and at night, in the silence of the palace, his voice could be heard sobbing, "What have I done? What have I done?"

A weak king implied a weak kingdom. The enemies of Kinda grew bold, and the plundering attacks of bandits became more and more frequent, while tribes battled for control of a territory that no one came forth to defend. Merchant caravans no longer passed through Dhat Kahal, and the kingdom inevitably grew poorer.

Walid knew very well what was happening in his kingdom, but he felt detached from it all, as though it had nothing to do with him. It didn't matter. Nothing mattered to him anymore, except for . . .

One winter afternoon when the king was seated by a window, toying absentmindedly with the key that concealed his most terrible secret, someone entered the chamber. Walid noticed nothing until a cough brought him out of his daydream. Before him stood a thin, long-faced man with a sharp and calculating look.

"You are well met, sire," he saluted him obsequiously. "As the great poet said, 'Thou art the sun, and all other kings are stars that disappear when the sun comes forth . . .'"

"I do not remember calling for you, Hakim," the king said indifferently.

"But sire, I only . . ."

"Go."

Unintimidated, the old *rawi* tried again:

"I will come to the point, sire. Everyone says that you are ill. I consider it my duty to inform you that, taking advantage of this belief, the vizier has taken power and is leading the kingdom to ruin."

Walid stared at Hakim. Whatever his subjects might think, he was still perfectly well informed of what was happening in his kingdom and his palace, and indeed he was more aware than anyone else of where his real troubles lay. He knew that the vizier was working hard to hold the kingdom together. Hakim's lie was so obvious that the king wondered how he could have listened to him for so long.

Hakim misinterpreted this look of astonishment.

"I realize that it is difficult for you to believe, sire, but it is true: I have seen for myself how this viper is robbing you of your power and using it to tyrannize your people. Such an act is high treason, and it deserves to be punished with death."

Walid was nearly speechless at his *rawi*'s audacity.

"Do you presume to tell me that I should execute my own vizier?" he said at last.

Hakim realized that he had been too blunt.

"No, certainly not; we all know your majesty's benevolent nature, like a great river that overflows its banks. . . ."

Hakim went on talking, but Walid did not listen. For the first time he saw his once inseparable companion for who he truly was: an unscrupulous rat who coveted the post of grand vizier of Kinda and would do anything to attain it. And he made what he later considered the first proper decision of his life. He stood up with some effort, fixed his gaze on his old *rawi*, and said:

"You are banished, Hakim, for conspiring against the life of an innocent man. I no longer wish to see you in my palace, nor anywhere in the kingdom."

Hakim stood openmouthed.

"But . . ."

"You heard me. Go at once or I will send my guards after you, and then there will be no mercy."

Hakim looked at him in amazement, and then with enmity and hatred. With an exaggerated, mocking bow, he left the room.

Walid felt a bitter sensation of victory. Hakim represented a part of his life he preferred not to remember, a series of mistakes he would not commit again. Walid ibn Hujr, king of Kinda, was going to change.

He made certain that his old *rawi* had left the palace, and then went to see the vizier.

He found him in the audience chamber, attending to the representatives of a Bedouin tribe reduced to misery by bandits. The vizier was sweating, his eyes sunken deep in his head. He was trying to explain that he wanted to help the tribe but could not: The kingdom itself was in ruins.

Walid grew even more remorseful. The vizier was a good man; he had served his father faithfully, and now he had taken on the weight of a responsibility that was not his own. Walid understood that many things in Kinda would need to be different, beginning with himself.

* * *

Walid left his confinement and tried to return to the center of political life. He discovered that great sums of money were needed to revitalize the kingdom, and he did not hesitate to open the royal treasure chambers.

Only one room remained closed. What was contained in it only the king knew, but it was rumored to be a magnificent treasure indeed. . . .

Slowly, Kinda rose out of its desperate situation, but the splendor and prosperity of its olden days never returned. Nor did Walid ibn Hujr ever regain the happiness and cheer of his youth.

*   *   *

The night was dark and moonless. Three figures slipped cautiously through the gardens of the royal palace, staying close to the walls.

One of them spoke in a low, faltering voice:

"You had better know what you're doing —"

"Shut your mouth," the man in front interrupted. "They'll hear us."

The three entered a side door, silent as ghosts. The guard who had once watched the door had left his post months before, in search of a better fortune in some other land, and one of the three men knew this.

They crept through the palace in darkness; to conserve oil, Walid had ordered that no lamps be lit while everyone was sleeping. Even so, the intruders' guide moved through the labyrinthine corridors with the greatest ease.

They descended several stairways before reaching their destination: the royal treasure chambers. They entered the rooms carefully. No one was guarding them.

"I don't like the look of this," one of the thieves said.

"Don't worry, Masrur," said the leader. "The king of Kinda is as poor as a rat. He doesn't need anyone to guard a treasure he doesn't possess."

"Then what are we doing here? You promised us wealth without end."

"Silence. I know things no one else knows. I know there's a secret room here below, and I have no doubt most of his ancient treasure is hidden inside it. No king would be stupid enough to spend it all just to feed his poor peasants."

The others made no further objection but followed their leader, who kept on without hesitation, confident of where he was going.

Finally they stood before a door that was shut tight and protected with a heavy chain. Hidden as it was in the dark, they would have passed it by if their guide had not stopped directly before it.

"Here it is," he whispered. "The great treasure of our good friend Walid." He turned to the third man in the group. "Suaid, you know your job."

The man he had called Suaid stepped forward, looking for something in his bag. He was the most skillful thief in all of Damascus. No lock or bolt could stop him. But he had not begun to work when a voice startled the three of them:

"Halt! What are you doing here?"

Out of the shadows came a rather sleepy and heavy-set guard, carrying a lamp in one hand and a formidable scimitar in the other. The leader of the thieves stepped forward fearlessly.

"Don't you recognize me, Jalaf?"

The guard looked at him with a perplexed expression.

"You! But what are you . . . ?"

He said nothing more. A dagger hidden up the thief's coat sleeve sprang out and plunged into the guard's heart, and he fell dead to the floor.

The other two were petrified. They were thieves, not assassins. They had followed their leader because of the promise of an easy strike. Killing someone had not been part of the plan.

The leader picked up Jalaf's lamp and turned toward them, still holding the bloody dagger.

"What about that lock, Suaid?" he said coldly.

*   *   *

Walid woke suddenly from a restless sleep, bathed in sweat. He woke frequently every night, but this time his eyes opened for a reason.

Someone had entered the storeroom that held the carpet.

He sat up and tried to calm himself — it had only been a dream. Yet it had seemed so real. . . .

He leaped up with a start and left his chambers at once. He needed to make sure that everything was all right.

*　*　*

The three thieves raised the lamp and looked around, expecting to see endless riches. All they saw was a carpet rolled in a corner.

"You tricked us," said Suaid, gritting his teeth. "There's nothing in here."

The leader leaned over the carpet, baffled and furious, and unrolled it partway. An ordinary wool carpet, not especially beautiful, although its design was very elaborate, and if one stared at it awhile, it even became disturbing. . . .

Suddenly they heard a muffled cry, and the three of them turned around as one.

It was Walid ibn Hujr, king of Kinda, barefoot and wearing his nightshirt, standing still and sorrowful over the body of his faithful servant Jalaf.

"I told you to stand guard, Suaid!" the leader muttered.

He had risen with a start, and by the light of the lamp Walid could see the man's face, pale and narrow and fox-like. Hakim.

Walid froze for a moment in shock.

But then Hakim cried, "Kill him, Masrur!" and the enormous Masrur advanced toward him with a club in his fist. Walid bent down to seize the fallen Jalaf's scimitar.

"Kill him!" Hakim repeated. His face had contracted into a hateful scowl. "It's the king!"

Masrur hesitated a moment, and Walid took advantage of this to lunge at him, but the thief dodged away.

"You are a foolish dreamer, Walid," Hakim said. "You always have been, and you always will be. A fainthearted man like you doesn't deserve to be king of Kinda."

His words were so full of venom that Walid turned to respond. Then something struck him on the head, and everything went black.

❊   ❊   ❊

"Sire . . . sire, wake up!"

Walid slowly opened his eyes and looked around in confusion. He made out the face of his grand vizier, who let out a sigh of relief.

"You're alive, sire! Thank goodness! When I saw poor Jalaf . . ."

"Jalaf . . ." Walid muttered.

He saw where he was, sprawled out on the floor of an underground chamber, next to the guard's bloody corpse. Then he remembered.

"The carpet!" he cried, sitting up suddenly.

Dizzy as he felt, he looked around the room, searching for his greatest treasure and his greatest curse. Nowhere could he see the last magnificent work of Hammad ibn al-Haddad.

"Sire!" the vizier groaned. "Don't do that; the blow to your head looks very bad. You are lucky to be alive."

He was right, Walid thought bitterly. He remembered the expression of deep hatred that Hakim had given him and wondered why the thief hadn't killed him. The king of Kinda doubted that it was good luck to still be alive. He jumped up in spite of the vizier's protests and, ignoring the pain, ran out of the room as quickly as he could.

In a moment he was at the stables, and without even gathering up provisions or putting on a *djellabah* and turban, Walid shot out of the palace at full gallop without looking back. Hatred and the desire for revenge did not drive him now. What tormented him was the weight of guilt, the remorse at having failed in his duty to repay the harm he had done to Hammad ibn al-Haddad: He was responsible for that strange and wondrous carpet, and it was his obligation to keep it from falling into the wrong hands. With the carpet lost, his palace and kingdom no longer mattered. His only obsession was to track down the three thieves, Masrur, Suaid, and his old apprentice and companion, Hakim.

Walid ibn Hujr, last king of Kinda, spurred on his horse without rest, all the stars of the universe shining over the desert and one idea hammering in his head: He must recover the carpet. He must.

8

THE BANDIT

He rode without stopping for three days and three nights under the blazing sun and the ice-cold moon, mad with fury and despair, disregarding hunger, thirst, heat and cold, his horse's exhaustion, and his own. Blind instinct led him on one certain course, and it never occurred to him to think that it wasn't correct.

But on the afternoon of the third day, at the hour of greatest heat, his horse collapsed and fell on the burning sand, and never stood up again.

Walid abandoned the horse and continued on foot, oblivious to walking barefoot, the soles of his feet on fire. He went on walking and walking, day and night, for several days more. One morning he stopped at last to study the horizon.

There was something up ahead that his tired and sunburned eyes couldn't make out clearly; a speck of red seemed to be moving toward him.

When his eyes focused, he saw that the speck was a red turban. It was still too far away for him to distinguish the features of the man wearing it, but Walid could see that he was small and somewhat stooped over, perhaps an old man.

He wondered in surprise what an old man was doing alone in the desert. It didn't occur to him that his own presence there might seem strange to anyone who saw him.

Walid moved toward the man in the red turban, but even after walking for some time, he was strangely unable to reach him. Instead of coming nearer, the old man kept getting farther away. Walid could follow him only so far.

He collapsed onto the sand, practically dead from exhaustion, just as his horse had done a few days before. His last thought was, *Forgive me, Hammad.* . . .

✻   ✻   ✻

Something brushed his face and neck, and Walid opened his eyes. It took an effort at first to remember even his own name. Before he could ask himself where he was and what had happened, a weather-beaten face with a thick black beard appeared before him.

But when Walid blinked the face disappeared, and once again he fell into a feverish daze.

He never knew how long he spent in this state. The periods of fever were mixed with times of wakefulness, and only now and then was he able to guess what was happening around him. He caught a glimpse of tent-cloth and heard the sounds of water and wind in the palm trees. And he often saw fleetingly the bearded face of the man who seemed to have saved his life.

*   *   *

One night, Walid opened his eyes clearly and looked about. Through the opening in the tent he saw a patch of starry sky and a bit of vegetation. Again he heard water flowing over rocks and the breeze in the palm trees, that gentle murmur that his father had loved so much. A little farther off, he could hear and see a crackling, glowing fire. He got up with an effort and stumbled outside, his body still weak.

The cool night air made him shiver as he approached the fire. Several other tents stood in the clearing, horses tied up nearby, but only the bearded man sat gazing intently at the flames. Walid sat down beside him, but he didn't even lift his eyes.

For a while, neither one spoke, until Walid broke the silence.

"Thank you for saving my life."

"It was nothing," the man answered.

Again they fell silent.

"Why did you do it?" Walid asked after a while.

[93]

The other man finally looked at him. By the light of the flames, Walid saw that the man was much younger than he had supposed — perhaps about twenty years old — and he was tall and strong, not small and stooped. He couldn't be the man in the red turban. Still, his weather-beaten face and calloused hands gave him the appearance of someone with great experience. His eyes glowed with intelligence and self-assurance.

"To tell the truth, I was curious," he said. "I wanted to know what a man was doing in the middle of the desert barefoot and dressed in his nightshirt."

Walid blushed and looked away.

"It's a long story. The truth is that I made most of the journey on horseback."

"A white horse, that you left dead more than five days from here?" The man shook his head in surprise. "It's still quite a feat. Tell me, my friend, is someone pursuing you?"

Walid thought for a moment. No one in his kingdom would have come this far in search of him. There was that strange old man in the red turban . . . but he had probably been a hallucination, or something Walid had seen in his dreams.

But as he shook his head, he remembered his mission, and looked at the man with a new light in his eyes.

"Have you by any chance come across three men carrying a carpet?"

"In the middle of the desert?" His rescuer laughed.

"But this is an oasis. . . ."

"A secret, lost oasis, my friend." A spark suddenly flashed in the young man's eyes. "They call me Sayf, and you've come to the spot where my people and I rest during hard times."

Walid recognized the name at once: Sayf meant *saber*, and this man was a *suluk*, a bandit, the fiercest who had ever laid siege to Kinda. He and his band had begun attacking the city several months before, and they had soon become the greatest worry of the king and his grand vizier. Walid knew that if he said who he truly was, Sayf would kill him with no hesitation at all.

"I am *al-Malik al-Dillil*, the Wandering King," he said cryptically.

Sayf laughed again.

"You've been sick a long time, my friend! There are no kings anymore. King Walid of Kinda was murdered some days ago when the Banu Asad attacked Dhat Kahal and set fire to the palace. No one survived. Nothing is left of the old kingdom now; each tribe has gone back to its own territory, and no one rules over anyone else."

Walid tried to hide his horror.

"You mean that the king was assassinated?"

"At night, by treason, from what I've heard. But not even he could have saved the kingdom from the Banu Asad. There were too many of them, and they were helped by dozens of smaller tribes. About time too — Kinda's been going to ruin for years."

Walid closed his eyes and rested his face in his hands.

"I see that the news has affected you," said Sayf. "I thought perhaps you were a survivor of that massacre."

Walid lifted his head. "Now that I know your hiding place, are you going to kill me?"

Sayf gave him an appraising look. Their eyes met.

"You're a strong and sturdy sort of man," he said. "Do you know how to use a sword?"

"Whenever you want, I can show you," Walid replied.

The *suluk* laughed again.

"I like that. So, seeing that you have a dark past, and that I have just saved your life, I'm going to make you a generous offer. Join up with us."

"I can't," Walid answered at once.

Sayf's expression hardened.

"You have until dawn to think it over, *Malik*." He pronounced Walid's improvised alias with a hint of mockery. "If you decide to join our company, we'll take you in like a brother. If not, I'll abandon you in the desert just as I found you. Fair enough, don't you think?"

Walid agreed without a word and walked off among the trees to think, his head spinning. If what the outlaw had told him was true, then everyone had given him up for dead and his kingdom no longer existed. He felt a stab of pain. If the Banu Asad had set fire to the palace, then the magnificent archive to which old Ibrahim and Hammad ibn al-Haddad had dedicated their lives must have burned along with it. If everyone was dead, then his faithful vizier had not been saved, nor the women of the harem, nor any of the servants whom he knew by name . . .

He had failed them all.

"I am a terrible king," he said aloud. "I've brought ruin to my kingdom, I've been cruel, arrogant, and jealous, and many people suffered and died because of me." Some part of him was happy, he realized, that everyone thought he was dead.

He considered Sayf's offer again. He could join this band of thieves and begin a new life, or he could go on being Walid ibn Hujr, lost in the desert, looking for the carpet. But even if he survived the desert alone, he hadn't the slightest idea where to begin his search. Hakim and his companions had a great advantage over him.

He breathed deeply and listened to the sounds of the oasis, a cool, refreshing place full of life and beauty. He came to the spring and studied his reflection in the water by the light of the moon and the stars. He didn't recognize himself. The man looking back at him seemed to be nothing at all like the proud young man who had once been the prince of Kinda.

When he returned to the tent, he knew for certain

that he would accept Sayf's offer. When he was king of Kinda, Sayf had been his enemy. Now that Kinda no longer existed, Walid could think of nothing more different from his former life than joining Sayf as a bandit.

Walid ibn Hujr, king of Kinda, was dead, and Malik, the *suluk*, the outlaw, had come to life.

* * *

He soon learned to love his new existence. For the first time Walid saw the realities of the world outside the palace, and he adopted the *suluk*'s motto: steal to live. Sayf's gang took pride in following the true bandit's code of honor, never killing innocent people, only attacking the warriors of other tribes in ambushes and robberies. In battle Walid's eyes flashed like his sword of steel, and his slender body soon bore countless scars. His inner rage emerged only when he fought for his life and his friends: cheerful Kab, enormous Akrasha, shrewd Hamid, and of course the leader, young Sayf, whose courage and determination knew no bounds.

Walid learned not only to respect and admire Sayf, but to love him like a brother. Sayf likewise grew devoted to this newest member of the company. Walid once saved his life during an ambush, and this strengthened the bond between them. They often went out riding together, usually without having to say a word.

On those travels, Walid learned to take in all of the desert like breath — its dunes and hills, its sparse vegetation, and the animals that lived in it, jackals, wild donkeys, and cattle. He came to love his proud black horse, and the true freedom that was his for the first time in his life. He finally understood the old verses that said, "The true bandit's face glows like a burning coal."

*   *   *

Months passed, and then a year. One night, watching the stars on a ride with Sayf, he found himself composing verses in his head to express their beauty. He smiled as he remembered al-Nabiga al-Dubyani's criticism. Would he be able to create a worthy *nasib* now that he had learned to love the desert?

But he realized at once that he was still far from the talent of great Hammad ibn al-Haddad, and it had been a long time since he had abandoned poetry. Walid ibn Hujr composed verses, but Malik, the *suluk*, did not.

He let out an almost imperceptible sigh that caught Sayf's attention.

"What are you thinking about, Malik?"

"I was thinking about poetry."

Sayf made a face of disgust.

"I don't trust poets," he declared. "They're full of jealousy and lies."

"Not all of them," Walid replied, remembering al-Nabiga and Hammad, "even though I know why you say so."

"Poetry is a terrible weapon in the hands of an unscrupulous man," said Sayf. "As the poet says, 'A wound from the tongue is like a blow from the hand.'"

"You speak against poetry, but you quote from poets to do it," Walid observed.

Sayf's eyes were lost in the stars.

"As a child, I wanted to be a poet," he said. "My father composed beautiful verses, and I wanted to learn from him. But I came to know a poet who was crueler than the bloodiest thief."

"You did?"

Sayf nodded.

"He killed my father. He subjected him to terrible tortures. His body arrived home in a cart like a load of cheap goods, led by a servant who didn't even know what he was carrying. He was in horrible condition, like someone who had spent a long time in prison. My poor mother died of sorrow."

Walid froze. He knew this story all too well.

"And all of this was done by a man who called himself a poet. He was jealous because my father had proven himself better in a competition."

Walid looked at his friend in a completely new light.

Those intelligent eyes, that resolute expression, that lean and supple body. How many years had passed since the tournament? Could it be . . . ?

"The gold my father won in the contest was meant to offer my brothers and me a better future," Sayf recalled. "In my case, it was useless. Months after my father's death, a rival tribe attacked our village and made off with everything. I became an outlaw to fight against King Walid and his men. I was sorry to hear he died, because then I couldn't kill him with my own hands."

These words confirmed Walid's worst fears. He knew he could no longer hide.

"What is your real name, Sayf?"

The *suluk* shot him a piercing look.

"No one who knew it has lived to tell."

"I know it." Walid pulled the reins of his horse to bring it closer to Sayf's. "You are Amir ibn Hammad, the son of the carpet weaver of al-Lakik."

Sayf pulled back, his eyes sharp as a sword blade.

"I see that my father's story is not unknown in the place you come from," he said coldly.

Walid looked at him, then dismounted with a leap and threw himself down on the sand.

"Kill me," he said with a choking voice. "I killed your father."

"You're lying, Malik. King Walid killed my father."

"I *am* King Walid. I'm the man you are looking for. I imposed terrible tasks on your father, and he accomplished them every time. It was my fault that he died exhausted — I forced him to spend all his genius on a carpet, one extraordinary carpet. . . ."

A change came over Sayf's face — Amir's face — as Walid spoke. He unsheathed his sword without taking his eyes off him.

"It's you, you damned traitor! You've changed a lot. And I took you in like a brother!"

"Kill me," begged Walid, still lying prostrate before him. "I don't deserve to live. Kill me and put an end to my cursed life."

Amir raised his sword, and Walid waited, but the chief *suluk* slowly lowered his weapon.

"First, tell me everything," he said hoarsely.

Walid felt that Amir had the right to know how his father had died, and he told him everything he didn't already know: Hammad's patient work in the archive, how Walid had imposed on him the task of weaving a carpet that contained the whole history of the human race, and how he had accomplished it, first losing his mind, then his sight, and finally, his life.

Amir listened, wide-eyed.

"He . . . accomplished it?"

"He did," murmured Walid. "Your father was an

extraordinary man, and I'm a miserable wretch to have destroyed him."

"You said you offered him his freedom and he refused it."

"I offered it to him too late. Too late. . . ."

He went on to tell how he had hidden the extraordinary carpet, neglected his rule over Kinda, and exiled Hakim; how Hakim had come back to steal the carpet, and how Walid had fled in search of him.

"Now you know," he concluded, "what a man like me was doing in the middle of the desert, barefoot and wearing nothing but a nightshirt."

Amir did not answer. He remained pale-faced, his eyes dark.

"Kill me," Walid pleaded.

The bandit turned toward him.

"I ought to do that," he said slowly, "and I would have done it the day I found you in the desert if I had known who you were. But now I know who you are, and you're not who you say you are."

Walid opened his mouth to protest, but Amir held up a hand.

"I knew Walid ibn Hujr, and he was a vain, egotistical, and cruel prince. But you are Malik the *suluk* — brave, generous, loyal, and above all, a man of honor."

Walid looked at him but did not understand. He

could see in Amir's eyes that his friend believed his story, and he felt more confused than before.

"I might be Malik the *suluk* now, but before I was Walid ibn Hujr, the prince and king of Kinda," he said. "I can change my name, but not my past. I was Walid ibn Hujr, and I committed terrible crimes. I killed your father, and I deserve to die for it."

"What you say is true," Amir agreed. "Believe me, I don't lack reasons to kill you. Still, something stops me from raising my sword against you: You once saved my life. For that, I am in your debt."

"You saved me first," Walid objected. "We are even now."

"I didn't do that out of friendship, and I would have left you where I found you if you had not decided to join us. I know what I'm saying. That time I saved a stranger, but you saved Sayf the *suluk*, just as I am sparing the life not of a stranger, but of Malik, or Walid ibn Hujr. And now, yes, we are even, according to the code of honor." Amir resheathed his sword. "Still, that does not mean I'm going to forget your story. I, Sayf, say this to you: There is no place for you among the *suluk* any longer."

For Walid, this sentence was worse than death.

"What must I do, then?"

"Go and do what you will, but know that if we ever meet again, I will show no mercy to the man who killed my father."

Walid was silent a moment.

"I understand," he said.

Neither one spoke as they returned to camp. Walid prepared to depart, packing provisions on his horse's back. He said no good-byes to Kab or Akrasha or Hamid, who were still sleeping, but after he mounted his horse, he turned to look at Amir ibn Hammad one last time.

"I am happy to see that Hammad lives on in you," he said.

Amir did not reply. Walid saw sadness and rejection in his eyes, but also compassion.

Without another word, he spurred his horse and left the oasis, fast as a ray of light under the starry sky.

9

THE BEDOUIN

As he rode his black horse across the desert, Walid thought about fate.

In years past he had believed his destined course was to become a great king, the greatest in Kinda's history — he possessed all the qualities he needed for it. He had dreamed too that part of that destiny was to be a famous poet, a man who won the competition in Ukaz for his skill with words and images.

But life was showing him that his fate lay elsewhere. And it seemed to be tied to that awkward old man who had proven, one bright day, that *he* was the greatest poet in Kinda. The day when Walid ibn Hujr's life took an unexpected turn.

My fate is in that carpet, he said to himself as he pressed his horse on. *I tried to ignore it by becoming Malik, the bandit, but it turned out that my friend Sayf was Amir ibn Hammad. It was a sign. I will find that carpet, because that is what my fate demands.*

But at other times he thought, *I could have kept silent and not revealed my identity to Hammad's son. Nothing would have changed. I would have gone on being a bandit. Walid ibn Hujr would have died once and for all. Nothing is forcing me to go off in pursuit of that carpet. And after all, maybe I have been acting out of pride, to pretend I am worthy of recovering it. How do I know that I am interpreting the signs correctly?*

Walid had always believed that one's fate is written down in advance — that one only had to follow a well-marked path — but now he saw that his own actions and decisions had led him to this situation. The awareness that he was responsible for what he had done woke powerfully inside him.

If fate is decided in advance, he thought, *why have my decisions changed my life so much? And if it isn't, why did I find Amir, when I thought my past had died along with my name?*

He had no answers, but he knew now what he was going to do: search for the carpet that Hammad ibn al-Haddad had woven, and come back to give it to his son, Amir, even if it cost him his life.

So on he rode. Arabia is a very large land, and the desert had long erased the footprints of the three thieves who had crossed it more than a year earlier. They could have fled to Persia, or Syria, or Egypt, or someplace even farther away.

Nevertheless, Walid suspected that they had headed north. Hakim had come to Kinda from a city in the north and might still have connections there. Moreover, the great stretch of desert that separated Kinda from other civilized kingdoms was only frequented by certain Bedouin tribes, and any traveler who dared to cross those parts would have to beg food and shelter from them sooner or later.

Walid was certain that in one of those tribes, someone would remember three men fleeing from Kinda with a carpet.

He had traveled for several days, seeking the shade of the hills and the small, refreshing oases, when he spotted a distant mountain range reaching to the sky, dividing the desert in two. Vegetation seemed to grow on its slopes, and Walid knew that he had chosen a good path.

He reached the foot of the mountains at midmorning, and after exploring the place for a while, he stopped to rest. There was surely a pass that crossed these mountains, but so far he hadn't found it. Walid wiped his brow, wondering whether he would have to go all the way around the mountains in the end.

"Good afternoon, stranger. May the *djinns* look on you with favor."

Startled, Walid turned around and saw a dark and wrinkled little man with a striking red turban on his head, sitting cross-legged on a flat rock.

Walid blinked.

"Good afternoon, stranger," the little old man repeated.

"Good afternoon," Walid felt obliged to answer.

He realized he was staring intently at the man and looked away in confusion. *A red turban is not so unusual,* he said to himself. *That old man I saw in the distance a year ago was just a hallucination.*

"I see you are looking for a pass through the mountains," said the old man. "The sons of the tribe of Bakr live on the other side. Are you sure you want to cross?"

Walid shrugged. "Why not?"

"In that case, go up this slope and you will find a road."

"I've done that already, old man. There's no road up there."

"That's because you haven't looked hard enough. I assure you that if you seek a road you will find it."

Walid did not wish to offend him, and it wouldn't hurt to go up there again, even though he knew he wouldn't find anything. So he left his horse grazing and climbed to the place that the old man in the red turban had pointed out.

He gave a quick look around, enough to make sure, and he was just about to go back down again when he saw it: a road through the mountains, narrow and partly hidden by rocks, but not so hidden that it would have escaped Walid's sharp eyes. *Strange*, he thought. *The old man was right. But how is it possible that I didn't see the pass before?*

He quickly went back to get his horse and his belongings, and saw that the old man in the red turban had disappeared. Walid looked around for him in vain; the man must have left in quite a hurry. Walid shrugged and climbed toward the pass once more, leading his horse behind him.

He crossed the mountains along the road, and as he descended the rocky crags, he heard the tinkle of water sliding over stones. His heart filled with joy. Until then he had found only shallow wells along the way, but in the mountains, the earth and sky gave the desert's children their most precious gift: water.

At the foot of the ridge, the stream spilled into a deep, glittering pool. His horse neighed in relief at the sight. He was a tough and mighty animal, but a march across the desert had left him at the end of his strength. Walid dismounted so both of them could enjoy their good fortune.

After drinking until he was satisfied, Walid stood up and surveyed their surroundings. The mountains were behind him now, a crest of rock battered by the desert sun and wind. Before him lay a grassy terrain with a little river flowing from the pool, and far to the north, a patch of green that seemed to be a small oasis.

Then he started; just on the other side of the water,

he saw a figure dismounting from a camel to let it drink from the stream. No doubt this was someone who had come from the oasis and could tell him what he would find there. Without hesitation, he crossed the stream and approached the stranger, who noticed his presence and rose in surprise. Walid hastened to show that his intentions were friendly.

"May the *djinns* look on you with favor," he called in greeting, using the phrase he had heard from the old man in the red turban.

The other didn't hear, or made no sign of it, but swung swiftly back onto the camel.

"Wait!" cried Walid. "I only want to know . . ."

But the rider spurred the camel away from him, shooting him only one quick glance. The face was covered, but in a fraction of a second Walid glimpsed the most beautiful eyes he had ever seen.

He stood still for a moment, watching the rider disappear into the distance in the direction of the oasis. Had he begun to hallucinate again? First the man in the red turban, and then those eyes. . . . He went to fetch his horse.

Soon they were on their way again, following the course of the river toward the oasis. Verdant pastures grew alongside the stream, protected by the mountains from sandstorms and the blazing sun. *A little paradise,* Walid thought.

Evening was coming on when he reached the oasis and spotted a camp set up in the abundant palm trees. It was much larger than the bandits' hideout he had shared with Sayf and his gang; there were several household tents and a number of enclosures for camels, horses, and even sheep. The tents were very large and divided into two sections, one for women and the other for men and their guests: an authentic Bedouin camp.

Walid approached slowly, facing the setting sun so that they could see him clearly. Two young men came up on horseback to meet him.

"Greetings, stranger!" one said. "What brings you to the tribe of Bakr, and what do you seek?"

"The legendary hospitality of the men of the desert," Walid replied. "I'm a weary traveler come from afar, and it seems I have found a place of peace in this valley."

The young men smiled in amusement, but led him to the camp and to the entrance of one of the tents. A man emerged; not very tall, but with a dark and deep-furrowed face, and with piercing eyes that commanded respect.

Walid dismounted and bowed, and the man bowed to him in answer.

"I am Sheik al-Harit," he said, "leader of the tribe of Bakr."

"I am honored," Walid replied.

"Who are you, stranger?"

"They call me *al-Malik al-Dillil*, the Wandering King."

"A most unusual name. Are you really a king?"

Walid thought of Kinda, and the news he had heard from Sayf a year before.

"No," he said, smiling sadly. "Only a fool, in search of something impossible."

The sheik looked at him curiously, but asked no more.

"If your intentions are friendly, you will find a place among us."

"They are," Walid said. "I will not refuse your hospitality, but neither will I trouble you for long. I only need some information, and I will be on my way."

Sheik al-Harit was silent a moment, then nodded slowly. "In that case, you should speak to the elders."

Walid agreed. He knew that among the Bedouins the elders were held in such high esteem that a sheik could make no important decisions without consulting them first. He did not want to rest or eat before talking to them, and so as soon as Walid tied up his horse, al-Harit led him to their tent. Walid bowed in respect, looking among them for the old man in the red turban, but he was not there.

"I am searching for three men carrying a carpet," Walid said. He described Hakim, Masrur, and Suaid, and their burden.

The elders nodded, but kept silent a long time. Finally, one said: "We have not seen three men, such as you speak of, yet your story recalls to us a man who came here one year ago. He seemed terrified, on the verge of losing his mind. He was carrying a carpet that he would not let out of his grasp."

Walid's heart leaped, and he tried to calm himself to listen further.

"We took him in," another elder continued. "At times he raved like a madman, and yet he seemed to be sane. One morning we found him dead. He had hanged himself from the tree in front of his tent. The carpet had disappeared."

"Is it possible that someone killed him?" Walid asked.

"It is possible. But we will never know."

Walid thanked them, excused himself, and went off to think.

The elders' story was not so strange to him, but if that man had been Hakim or one of his henchmen, where had the other two gone? What had become of the carpet? *Perhaps I should wait for another sign,* he told himself. *It makes no sense to keep crossing the desert without a destination.*

He returned to the camp as a cry of alarm broke out: "The Taglib! The Taglib are attacking us!"

And he saw dozens of Taglib warriors rushing toward the camp from the mountains, even as the men of the tribe of Bakr climbed on horseback to defend their people.

Walid didn't hesitate. He ran to the camp, leaped onto his black horse, and joined the Bakr, hurling war cries and waving his sword in the air.

He soon found himself in the middle of the fight. Swords spun and danced, gleaming with blood, and cries of rage and pain mixed with the neighing of horses and the clashing of steel. In the heat of battle, Walid forgot his past and future; there was only this people who had taken him in and who were under attack. It did not cross his mind that the Taglib would doubtless have welcomed him with the same hospitality if he had come to their camp instead — the Bedouins do not distinguish between good and evil, but between honor and dishonor. Nor did he reflect that he did not even know what this battle was about. Once more his heart stirred with the joy of being part of something, and for Walid ibn Hujr, there was nothing but the present moment.

Night had fallen when the Taglib retreated in defeat to their territory on the other side of the mountains. The Bakr sent up savage cries of victory and returned to camp covered in sweat and blood.

That night they celebrated by the fire, Walid among them. Drunk with the glory of battle, he even composed and recited a poem in praise of the tribe of Bakr that was loudly applauded by all the Bedouins.

"Your eloquence is admirable, friend Malik!" the sheik declared with satisfaction.

Walid replied, "The poet said, 'The tongue is half of a man, and the other half is his heart. What remains is flesh and blood.'"

"Well, if only a tongue like yours had come along in our last fight against the Salaman! Curse me if they didn't carry off ten camels in revenge for the death of three of their mangy horses! The *djinns* did not favor us that day."

Walid laughed, but al-Harit looked at him in earnest.

"You are one of us now, Malik," he said. "I am proud to welcome you to my clan as a son, because you have taken up your sword in service of the Bakr, and fought with courage, and shed your blood for us."

Walid smiled in appreciation. He looked at the Bedouins gathered around the fire, men, women, and children. He saw that they were all family, and he felt envious. It was often lonely in the desert.

He noticed movement nearby, and as he turned, he saw a pair of eyes that he knew already, deep and dark as the Arabian night sky. This time he could also see a small mouth that smiled pleasantly, a graceful nose, a dark-skinned face, and a few curls of black hair.

"I know you," he said. "I saw you this afternoon by the stream."

But she pretended not to have heard.

"Welcome to the clan, brother," she said. "My name is Zahra."

"A beautiful name for a beautiful desert flower," he whispered, smiling in return.

"Zahra bint al-Harit," she said, and Walid's smile widened. He looked at her closely. In the harem of the palace of Kinda, he had no doubt known women more beautiful than this, but none of them mattered at all compared to her. Zahra met his glance and, without the slightest embarrassment, fixed her dark eyes on his.

"Will you stay with us?" she asked.

Walid looked toward Sheik al-Harit, wondering whether he would get into trouble by speaking so openly with the man's daughter. He knew that the Bedouins zealously protected their women from strangers.

"My father says that you are a good warrior," she added, guessing his thoughts. "He also says that you've lost the trail of something you're searching for."

Walid turned to her. "I don't know yet what I will do," he answered cautiously.

Yet he knew, deep in his heart, that he wanted to stay with them. With her.

*   *   *

He adapted to the Bedouins' customs just as he had adjusted to the ways of Sayf and his people. Despite the war with the Taglib, which had gone on for countless generations, life was more peaceful with the Bakr than among the thieves. The men of the tribe were more herdsmen than warriors, more practiced with camels and shepherds' crooks than with horses and swords.

Walid's way with words earned the Bakr great victories

in tribal disputes; soon he came to be known by the name of *al-Ajtal*, the Eloquent One, and in appreciation, al-Harit gave him a pair of camels with which to start his own flock. So Walid befriended a quiet, easygoing shepherd named Hasan, who taught him the job until he was ready to go off on his own.

Sometimes, roaming the mountainsides with his camels in search of pasture, Walid thought about fate once again. His days in the palace as prince and heir of Kinda seemed very far away. He often wondered whether it had been a dream, whether he hadn't been born in the desert in a dusty tent, swaddled in animal skins, instead of lying in a silk-covered cradle in the finest room of a palace.

Taking care of his flock, he found himself deeply moved the first time his she-camel gave birth. Although he rose up to defend his clan whenever necessary, he began to see that he loved life more than death, that he did not wish to go on killing.

When he was a prince, he had been taught that there was no life more important than his own, except for the king's. When he became a bandit he learned that the law of survival meant killing one's enemies, because it was the only way to live in an uncertain world. But now that he was a Bedouin, he discovered that every member of the clan had a name and a face, including the women and children — two groups the thieves had never noticed.

And he saw that if each life was individual, then each life was important. There were ways to survive without having to kill.

When the pastures had withered, the clan took down their tents, packed up their belongings, and set off across the desert, searching for another place to settle. Driven by the quest for pastureland, the Bedouin shepherds never stayed in one place for long. Each tribe had its own more or less established set of fields; in fact, Walid gathered that the war against the Taglib had begun over the ownership of an especially fine territory, the control of which hadn't been settled yet.

"In the desert there are few good pieces of land," Hasan said one day as they watched their flocks together. "Every one of them is important. Without good grass for our camels, we couldn't survive."

Walid understood. Even though the Bedouins lived at the edge of the desert, in the milder climate of the mountains, it wasn't an easy life.

Yet he saw that he had grown used to camels and tents and the nomadic way. He wondered whether his destined course wasn't to stay with the Bakr as a herder of camels. Among them he had come to feel part of a family, and found peace, and also . . .

Zahra had become a star within his heart, his reason to wake every morning at dawn. They often went out riding in the afternoon; at night they sat together by the fire, talking on and on. Each felt something for the other, but although al-Harit did not look unfavorably on them, Walid wanted to increase his flock again before he asked for Zahra's hand.

Toward the end of his fourth journey with the tribe in search of pasture, Walid went off with his camels to explore the new territory. He came upon Hasan's flock beside a creek. The shepherds waved to each other in greeting. Walid had learned that Hasan was a man of few words, but he liked him and knew he could confide in him. He sat down on the ground beside his friend.

"This is a good place here," Walid said after a while. "My speckled camel will be able to give birth in peace."

"And then you can talk to al-Harit about Zahra," Hasan added suggestively.

Walid blushed. "Is it so obvious?"

Hasan did not answer, but his silence said enough. Walid asked nervously:

"Do you think that al-Harit will say yes?"

Hasan smiled, but again did not answer. He knew very well what worried his friend. Even though he had been accepted into the clan, he was an outsider. Maybe he was being too bold in asking for the sheik's daughter as his companion.

"I know how you feel," Hasan said. "I too was adopted into the clan, some time ago."

Walid looked at him in surprise. It was true that

Hasan had different features, a fairer complexion and lighter hair than the rest of the Bakr, but it had never occurred to him that he was an outsider.

"Once they accept you, it is for better or worse, Malik," Hasan went on. "It's the bond of the *asabiyya*, the Bedouin solidarity. Now you are one of the clan, like their own flesh and blood."

"Did you come from far away?" Walid asked.

"Far enough to consider myself a stranger," he said. "I sold my flock of sheep to buy a pair of camels and join the Bedouins. I know it seems strange, but when I was a boy, my family was taken in by one of their tribes on our journey to Kinda, and ever since I had wanted to be a shepherd and live like them. So I left my own people to fulfill a dream."

"They must have mourned your departure," Walid said. "Have you gone back to see them?"

"No. But I have never regretted it. My father did everything possible to obtain the money I needed to buy a flock, and I would be unworthy of his efforts if I didn't make good use of the gift."

Walid's heart began to beat faster, although he did not know why.

"Tell me: What kind of work did your father do?"

"He was a carpet weaver. Why?"

"No reason," he whispered. "Have you heard any news of him recently?"

"I learned that al-Lakik, the place where my family lived, suffered an attack, and from what they said, no one survived."

Walid was quiet a long while. So was Hasan. They drank in a silence as full of meaning as the most intimate conversation, and then Walid said: "Yes, someone survived, Hasan. I knew your younger brother, Amir."

Hasan turned to him. "Little Amir? Do you mean . . . ?"

"Not so little anymore." Walid smiled. "Now he's a man, a brave man. They call him Sayf, and he's the leader of a gang of thieves."

Hasan fell silent again, taking in this news. Walid waited, not hurrying him. He was unafraid of confessing his disgrace — he was beginning to accept responsibility for his actions. Still, Hasan was a happy man, and he did not want to trouble him with bad news.

"My brother is alive," the shepherd mused.

"Will you go to see him?"

"I don't know," he said. "I'm a peaceful man and I've gotten used to this tribe. I don't know if I would dare set off on a journey across the desert alone."

"If you do," Walid persisted, "and if you finally find your brother, tell him for me that Malik was here with you. And that I have received a second sign that I must keep going to live out my destiny. That I'm going in search of what I lost, and that if I find it, he will hear news from me, because I'm not afraid of death anymore."

Hasan looked at him in amazement.

"You mean to say you're leaving us?"

Walid nodded.

"When I was younger, I committed many crimes, Hasan. I vowed to repair these wrongs, but twice now I have come close to backing out. I won't do it again."

Hasan was silent. Then he said: "We have never asked about your past, Malik. The Bedouins know how to read a man's soul in his face. And we saw a noble soul in you. Tormented, but noble."

"I have to make up for the harm I've done," Walid insisted.

"We won't prevent you. But what about Zahra?"

A storm of contradictory feelings encircled Walid's heart. "I don't deserve her," he declared at last, hoarsely. "Her father should marry her to someone of his own blood."

Hasan turned away and said nothing.

Walid went to speak with Sheik al-Harit and told him what he had told Hasan. Al-Harit listened to him gravely, and when Walid had stopped speaking, said simply:

"My daughter loves you, Malik."

Walid felt his throat go dry.

"And I love her in return. But I have a debt to repay, and until I repay it, I won't deserve to look into her eyes."

Al-Harit studied him for a long time, then rose, came forward, and embraced him.

"Good fortune to you, my son," he said. "May the *djinns* guide you on your way."

"Thank you, Father," Walid answered.

He left the tent and collided at once with Zahra, who had been listening to them in secret. Her dark eyes were full of tears.

"I am sorry," Walid murmured, and he went quickly away.

It did not take him long to gather his belongings. In a small sack he kept what little gold was left from his days with Sayf. He decided to leave his black horse with the tribe, and chose the best camel of his flock for the long journey that awaited him. As he mounted the animal for his departure, he saw something that made his heart turn over.

The Bedouins had gathered to say farewell. Next to al-Harit was Zahra. She was wearing clothes for the journey and had packed her belongings onto her own camel. Walid could read the determination in her eyes and looked at the sheik questioningly. The man shrugged.

"You cannot tame a desert wind," he said. "And you cannot hold back a woman who has chosen a man."

10

THE MADMAN

Zahra's presence at his side made the farewell less painful — it meant that he was not breaking all ties with the tribe of Bakr. It pleased him to imagine that he would return with her one day and stay among the Bedouins forever. But in moments of clarity he remembered that as soon as he recovered the carpet and brought it to Amir, its rightful owner, Amir would kill him. Yet he sometimes thought, *Now that I have met Hasan, I could return the carpet to him, since he is Hammad's son too.*

But despite all the choices he had now, he began to regret accepting Zahra's company by the time they camped at nightfall. As he studied the young girl's face in the light of the campfire, composing verses in his head in praise of her beauty, he felt that even though she was no doubt as tough and courageous as any woman of the desert, he had no right to place her in danger by forcing her to join his impossible search.

"I think you should return to your people, Zahra," he told her.

She looked up at him.

"Why? I won't be a burden."

"I know. But you won't have an easy life with me."

"That doesn't frighten me. I wasn't born to have an easy life."

Walid looked at her again, admiring her courage. She was young and slender, but in her eyes shone the fearlessness of a great warrior. As he studied her, he remembered al-Nabiga al-Dubyani's words so many years ago: "Your verses showed that you have never loved a woman." *How right he was,* Walid thought with a smile.

And for that very reason, because he loved Zahra so, he could not allow her to go on with him. He tried to dissuade her:

"I don't even know which way to go. I'm searching in the dark."

"And what are you searching for, if I may ask?"

Walid hesitated. He had never told anyone but Amir the whole story, and Amir had nearly killed him for it. If he told Zahra about his past life, she would probably not believe him, and if she did, she would want to have no more to do with him. That would be a good way of making her go home, although it meant that she would tell the truth to al-Harit, and Walid would lose a family once more.

"If I tell you, you won't believe me."

"If you tell me the truth, I will."

"But then I will lose you forever."

"You must take that chance."

"All right, I will." Walid took a deep breath. "My real name is Walid ibn Hujr, king of Kinda."

Zahra did not move, and her face showed no emotion. "Kinda no longer exists, and its king died with it."

"Yes and no. I caused the destruction of my own kingdom, but my days did not come to an end."

He told her of his kingdom, his palace, his father. He explained how he had organized three poetry competitions so that he could go to Ukaz, and how a humble weaver of carpets had beaten him every time. He described how he had wanted to ruin this man. He spoke of the archive of old Ibrahim, and the carpet that contained the history of the human race. He recounted Hakim's betrayal, and how the three thieves had made off with the carpet. He told her of his search, of Sayf who had been revealed as Amir ibn Hammad, of destiny and the signs of fate. He said that Hasan had turned out to be the carpet weaver's second son, and so he had had to abandon the tribe and continue his journey.

All this he explained to her, and as the words flowed from his mouth with characteristic ease, he felt the burden in his heart grow lighter.

When he finished speaking, he looked at her expectantly, studying her expression. But Zahra's face remained impenetrable.

"So, Walid ibn Hujr," she whispered. "I always thought that you spoke too well to be some wandering *suluk*. But I wouldn't believe it if I didn't know that your story was true."

"How could you know that?" Walid asked in surprise.

"Because when a sick traveler comes to our clan, it's the women who take care of him. The men often forget that, and they almost never ask us questions."

"What do you mean?"

"That I know this thief of yours, the man who stole the carpet and then killed himself. Only a few of us women remember his name. He was called Masrur. He was big and strong, but he was sick. Soon we realized that the illness wasn't in his body, but in his mind. He was delirious most of the time, but in one of his lucid moments he sent a message."

"A message?" Walid repeated.

"Masrur did not know how to read or write, so he dictated it to a messenger. We never knew what the message said, because the boy who carried it died a few days later in a battle against the Taglib. But the message must have reached its destination, because soon afterward a man arrived at the camp who claimed to be his friend. Masrur gave him the carpet and the man went off the way he had come. That night, Masrur killed himself."

Walid listened in disbelief.

"Why didn't the elders tell me this?"

"Because they didn't know. The stranger arrived in a caravan, and it's difficult for the elders to take notice of all the members of a caravan."

"And how do you know about it?"

"Because Suleima heard the two of them talking, and saw how the man left with the carpet. Later she told Azza, and Azza told me."

Walid felt more and more afraid.

"What kind of man was he? Was he tall, slender, with a long face?"

"I would say he was a small man. I remember that Suleima told Azza he could barely carry the carpet."

"It must have been Suaid," Walid muttered. "He took it. They split up, believing that I would send the guard after them. And that's just what I should have done," he groaned, "instead of running after them myself."

Zahra looked at him.

"And still I wouldn't have believed you if I hadn't seen and heard Masrur myself." She trembled. "I remember the things he said when he was delirious. He talked about that carpet as if some kind of curse were on it."

Walid was silent. Then he said:

"But I have to find it. The trouble is that we don't know where Suaid went."

"He came from Dumat al-Gandal. That's where young Salí carried Masrur's message."

"Dumat al-Gandal," Walid repeated.

"I could lead you there. I know the way."

Walid looked at her.

"Why do you want to go with me?"

"For a few reasons, not all of them having to do with you," she replied. "In the first place, I want to see the world. I want to know the great cities of the north, like Palmyra and Damascus. I want to visit the marketplace of Yathrib and the temple of Kaaba in Mecca. I want to see the gardens of the south, and to go even farther beyond, if my fate allows."

"But now you know who I was. Doesn't that matter to you?"

"I know who you were, and I know who you are. Of course it's important. You owe a debt, and you won't be free until you repay it. And I want a free man at my side. That's why I will help you find that carpet, Walid."

All of this was so strange to Walid: hearing his real name again after such a long time, her decision to go with him, the fact that she believed him.

"You are an extraordinary woman," he said.

"All women are," she answered with a smile. "But there is another reason."

"What is that?"

"The carpet. It tormented that man so much that he took his own life. It's something very uncommon, perhaps very dangerous. It has to be found."

Walid agreed.

"And there's one last reason," Zahra added.

"What is that?"

"That I love you. Of course."

✳ ✳ ✳

After two weeks of travel, they arrived in Dumat al-Gandal. It was a small village beside an oasis, which made Walid glad, because it wouldn't take long to uncover some trace of Suaid if he had passed through. They soon learned they had come to the right place.

"Suaid?" said old Butayna. "Listen to me, young man: Don't ask about him. Poor Abda!"

They received the same kind of answer from five different people, but finally they were shown to the house where Suaid lived with Abda, his wife, a small thin woman with a bitter look and sunken eyes.

"What do you want?"

"Does Suaid live here?"

"No." And the woman closed the door in their faces. Walid called out again.

"Madam, we have urgent business with Suaid."

"No one has urgent business with him!" came the reply from within.

"I do. It's about a carpet he took from Kinda. . . ."

They heard a stifled gasp, then silence. They waited.

"Maybe you shouldn't have mentioned the carpet," Zahra said.

"Perhaps," Walid began, but suddenly the door opened and they heard a cry.

Zahra and Walid leaped back, and this may be what saved their lives, because Abda threw herself toward them brandishing an enormous saber. Yet the weapon was too heavy for her, and after aiming a blow and missing, she lost her balance and fell.

Quickly Walid and Zahra held her down and took the saber.

"We only wanted to talk," Zahra said gently. "We didn't come to harm you."

"The carpet is mine," Walid announced. "Suaid and his accomplices stole it from the place where I was keeping it out of sight, the place where it should return."

Abda said nothing, but she stopped struggling, and tears filled her tired eyes. Walid and Zahra let her go, keeping close hold of the saber. Abda rose. Then, opening the door to the house, she said only, "I warn you."

Walid and Zahra entered cautiously. The room was dark; the only window had been covered with mats so that sunlight barely came through. Even so, they could tell there was no furniture inside, nothing but a plain straw bed in one corner.

"They came . . . they came at night. . . ."

The voice startled them. Looking around, they saw a human form pacing up and down against the wall like a caged lion.

"Suaid?" Walid asked hesitantly.

"Ships . . . fire. . . . No, the village was destroyed . . . the city too . . . we built temples . . . and looked for caves to live in . . . crossed the ocean. . . . But the whole world had been destroyed . . . no one was left, just a speck of dust in space. . . ."

"Suaid?" Walid repeated uneasily.

"War!" Suaid howled, making the visitors step back. "Liberty, equality, fraternity . . . Many, many people. They are born, they die, they live, all at once, all at the same time. . . ."

Walid shivered. This poor madman's senseless talk brought confused images to his mind that he would rather forget — they had nearly driven him mad too some time ago. Images in a many-colored carpet . . .

"Suaid, do you remember me? I am King Walid."

Suddenly the madman stopped and seemed to look at them.

"Hundreds of kings," he said. "Thousands of kings. One more, one less."

"You mustn't dare mention the carpet," Zahra whispered to Walid.

He had not thought of doing so.

"Do you remember Hakim and Masrur?" he asked Suaid.

"Hundreds of Hakims. Hundreds of Masrurs. I remember all of them. I don't remember any of them. The world is big and old."

"Hakim and Masrur, the thieves," Walid insisted.

"Thieves!" Suaid cried out, making the others step back. "Thieves stealing gold, stealing jewels, stealing women, in temples and houses and palaces. . . ."

"In palaces," Walid interrupted. "Thieves stealing in palaces. Hakim and Masrur and Suaid."

Suaid paused, disconcerted. It seemed that he was trying desperately to think, but the phrases that came out of his mouth made no sense.

"Palaces on the other side of the sea. Thieves, barbarians. They took my bridal gown, but . . . Hakim, water the horses! Please, sir, we are looking for Buckingham Palace. Can you tell us where . . . ? Tomb raiders! Masrur wanted to travel in space. He took his wife with him in the ship and . . . Look, the kings are coming back to the palace in a carriage! Thieves in the museum. Hakim, Hakim, Hakim, where do I begin?"

Suaid sobbed, defeated and desperate, and cowered in a corner. But Walid was running out of patience, and he stepped forward.

"Suaid, I am Walid ibn Hujr, king of Kinda. Hakim, Masrur, and you robbed my palace. You took" — he hesitated a moment before adding — "a carpet. A carpet . . ."

"A television," Suaid corrected him, trembling and weeping in a corner. Walid did not know any such word. "An eye that sees everything. No!" he shrieked. "Why do I have to remember? Everything and nothing! Nothing! Let me forget! I want to forget!"

"But the carpet . . ."

"Go away!" Suaid howled, holding his head in his hands. "Go away, impossible people! Go back to your hell, all of you, all of you! Thousands and millions of people visiting my dreams . . . saying and doing things I don't understand . . . things I remember and don't remember. . . ."

He fell silent. Walid felt sorry for the poor man, but he was afraid of what all this meant.

"Suaid, I'm sorry," he whispered.

"Let's go to the *agora*," he answered. "A great philosopher is speaking there today."

"What?" Walid asked.

"You don't understand me, sir. I have nothing left. It froze this spring, and the harvest. . . . But look over there! It's one of those machines they call automobiles. . . ."

Walid shook his head and stood up, going back to Zahra's side.

"Let's go," he said, and she agreed. But as they left the room, they heard Suaid's voice again.

"He's saying that the earth revolves around the sun — crazy, isn't it? You're right, he deserves to be burned. But the fact is that we've colonized Mars now, and our machines . . ."

"How did he reach such a state?" Walid asked, once the door was closed again.

Abda breathed deeply, rubbing her tired eyes. Behind her, Zahra moved quietly in the outdoor kitchen, preparing tea.

"He came with this cursed carpet," Abda remembered. "It seemed so vulgar. Elaborate and pretty enough, but no more than what you'd find in any bazaar in Persia. Yet for him, it was something extraordinary. I asked him about the treasure I assumed he'd brought, and he answered that this carpet was greater than a hundred treasures, and that the fool Masrur hadn't had enough sense to understand what he'd seen. He shut himself in with that carpet. He spent days and nights studying it, as if he saw great wonders there. It didn't take him long to confuse his own life with the lives he thought he could see in the carpet. Soon enough, he lost his mind, and ever since, everyone in al-Gandal calls him *al-Maynun*, the Madman."

"Was what he saw so terrible?" Zahra asked.

Abda accepted the cup of tea she offered her, but did not raise it to her lips.

"I don't know whether it was terrible," she said, "because I never dared look at it for long. For Suaid it was a marvel. It didn't frighten him to see things he didn't understand; everything about it fascinated him. He said that there were miracles and wonders we couldn't even dream of. I never knew what he meant."

"It's said that within this carpet is the entire history of the human race," Walid whispered.

"I don't know about that, but I believe he saw too much. So much that his mind couldn't bear it."

"Yes," Walid agreed. "When I asked him about Hakim he seemed confused, as if he knew so many Hakims that he didn't know where to start."

Silence fell. All that could be heard was the incomprehensible muttering from the other side of the wall.

"We were supposed to return to Damascus with the great treasure that Suaid promised," Abda sighed. "But we haven't been able to leave the village ever since this cursed carpet entered our house."

Walid shook his head. He felt he had reached the end of his journey, but he was still unsure what to do with Hammad's carpet once it was in his possession.

"It's still here, isn't it?"

The woman laughed bitterly.

"No, sir, it's not. Hakim came and took it away. I

didn't stop him — why should I? I didn't want that carpet in my house anymore, and besides, Hakim deserves
the same fate as Suaid. My husband was a thief, but he
never killed anyone. Hakim seemed like a very bad sort."

Walid felt as if cold water had been poured on his
head. Hakim, his old *rawi* and companion, the one he
thought was a friend, the traitor he had wanted to kill —
why hadn't he done it?

"Do you have any idea where he went, Abda?"

Her tear-swollen eyes met his firm gaze.

"Toward Damascus, to seek protection from the
brotherhood of thieves. And if he didn't go mad or kill
himself, that's where he must be."

11

THE SERVANT

Damascus was a colorful and bustling city, full of people, sounds, and smells — truly a feast for the senses. Zahra and Walid kept close together as they led their camels through the crowd. Zahra looked wide-eyed at everything, but didn't dare linger anywhere. Walid moved at a quick and confident pace, scrutinizing the streets with the eyes of a hawk. At last he paused and signaled for her to stop.

"We've found it, Zahra," he told her. "Exactly where Abda said it would be: the Red Camel."

Zahra saw a grimy-looking den with a camel the color of blood drawn beside the door. Nothing was written on it; no other sign was necessary.

"Wait here," Walid said.

She did not protest. Someone had to wait with the animals, and since Walid spoke many languages, it made sense for him to go in and inquire. But she also knew he would not want to make her set foot in such a place.

Inside, the Red Camel was exactly what it seemed from the outside — a filthy, dark, and foul-smelling tavern where the dregs of Damascus met. With his ragged appearance — obviously a man who had just come in from the desert — Walid stood out strongly there, and he soon felt hostile and suspicious glances directed his way.

The owner of the tavern hurried toward him, looking equally distrustful.

"What do you want, stranger?"

"I'm looking for a man who calls himself Salut the Trickster," Walid said, as Abda had instructed him.

"I don't know him," the tavern-keeper answered with a frown.

Having expected this, Walid quickly slipped one of his last gold coins into the man's hand.

"Wait, now I remember. . . ." The tavern-keeper turned toward a darkened part of the room. "Ask him over there. He might be able to tell you something."

Walid saw a little man seated in a corner — a dull and unremarkable sort that no one would look at twice. Still, he did not want to be fooled again; he remembered very well what a grave mistake it had been to underestimate Hammad ibn al-Haddad.

He sat across from the man and discreetly set a coin down before him.

"What do you want?" the man whispered.

"I'm looking for Salut the Trickster."

"What for?"

"I need some information."

"About what?"

"About someone."

"If that's all you're going to say, I can't help you."

"I'm only going to talk to Salut himself."

"Then start talking. I'm the one you're looking for."

Walid paused and looked at the man more carefully. He could guess why people called him "trickster" — his face was so plain and ordinary that it would be hard to remember.

"They tell me you know all the thieves in Damascus."

"Could be," he said, draining his cup in one swallow.

"I'm looking for one in particular, a man named Hakim. He came to the city two or three years ago. He once served as a *rawi* in the court of the king of Kinda."

Salut let out a short laugh.

"Nobody who's lived in a palace ends up in the alleys of Damascus dealing with thieves, know what I mean?"

Walid smiled to himself.

"Sure I do."

"All right, then. I don't know the man. But maybe you should ask al-A'sa. He's the one who controls this side of town."

"A blind man?" Walid asked in surprise, since that is what the name *al-A'sa* meant.

"Never underestimate a blind man, my friend. He's sharper than you'll ever be."

"Can you lead me to him, then?"

The little man smiled again.

"No. He doesn't let himself be seen very often, understand? It's bad for business. A lot of people would like to see him dead, know what I mean?" Walid nodded. "But if I see him, I'll ask him about this Hakim of yours. What's your name?"

"Malik."

Walid gave a full description of his old *rawi*, just as he recalled him. Salut promised to bring him news the next day.

Walid left the tavern feeling somewhat doubtful. Zahra was waiting outside with the camels, a questioning look in her dark eyes. They found an inn for the night, and he told her everything.

*　　*　　*

The next afternoon he found Salut in the same dark corner.

"Sorry, but I haven't had any luck," he said. "There's a Hakim Mustafá who grew up here in Damascus, but he's never been to Kinda. Besides, he's short and fat."

"He's not the one I'm looking for," said Walid in disappointment, and, not wishing to stay in that place a moment longer, he paid Salut and left. He took a long walk through the city streets, deciding what his next move would be. If Hakim hadn't joined the thieves in Damascus, where could he have gone?

It was night by the time he turned back toward the inn; Zahra would be waiting for him. He entered the winding alleyways with a sigh.

Suddenly he saw a flash of light out of the corner of his eye, but before he could draw his sword, six or seven people were upon him.

Walid fought fiercely, struggling for his life, but the strangers disarmed him and beat him badly. Lying bloody and wounded in the dust, he could barely hear his attackers whispering impatiently:

"Do you have the money?"

"Yes, yes, here it is . . . just a little bag, nothing else."

"There's got to be more. Keep looking."

He felt hands searching inside his clothing and tried to turn over, but one of the thieves jumped on his leg, and Walid cried out in pain as the bone broke. Then the thief jumped on his other leg.

"Damn it, Labid, stop playing and kill him!"

Walid saw a sword blade gleam next to his body. He closed his eyes.

Suddenly a voice came thundering down the alley:

"Get out of here, you sons of whores! May the *djinns* confound you!"

Walid fainted.

✳ ✳ ✳

He remained unconscious for several days. When he opened his eyes at last, he found himself on a humble but clean bed in a high-ceilinged room with white walls. A middle-aged woman with a kindly face was sitting beside him.

"Rest, stranger. You are in good hands."

"Where am I . . . ?"

"In the house of a powerful man who has taken you in until you recover. You're fortunate that Karim and his men passed down the alleyway that night. They saved your life."

"Who is Karim?" Walid managed to ask.

"I am," came a loud voice from the doorway.

Walid saw an enormous, muscular man with gold rings in his ears and a powerful set of teeth that flashed when he smiled. He vaguely reminded Walid of his friend Akrasha the bandit.

"I am the overseer of the house of Mr. Raschid, stranger," he declared. "My boys and I saved you. An old man in a red turban told us that a bunch of street rats were roughing up a poor Bedouin in an alley, so we stepped in. Too bad they got away, and we weren't able to get your belongings back."

"They weren't much," Walid whispered. "I'm grateful to you, Karim."

But then he shook his head in confusion. What was that about an old man with a red turban?

"How long have I been here?"

The woman smiled. "Oh, just five days, and when you got here you were practically dead."

"Only a man from the desert would think of walking through the worst part of Damascus at night. You are lucky to be alive, stranger."

Walid barely heard them. "Zahra!" he cried out. "She's waiting for me. . . ."

He tried to sit up, but could not. He looked down in horror at his legs, which were wrapped with splints.

"They broke your legs, the scoundrels," the woman said. "Too bad they escaped. Karim would have given them what they deserved."

"You bet I would, Abla."

Neither of them paid heed to Walid's distress or to his desperate efforts to get up.

"You don't understand!" he nearly shouted. "Zahra is my companion. She's waiting for me all alone. She'll know something terrible has happened. She'll come looking for me."

He pulled himself to the edge of the bed as well as he could, but lost his balance and fell to the floor with a crash.

"Careful, you'll hurt yourself even more!" Abla cried out in alarm.

"All right, all right," Karim grunted. "I will go looking for your woman."

The news he brought back worried Walid terribly. According to the innkeeper, Zahra had waited for Walid for two days, then gathered her things and left. She had not returned.

"She must have gone looking for me at The Red Camel," Walid muttered. "Damn it, I have to find her."

He managed to convince Karim to put him on a stretcher and have him carried at once to the tavern.

"A dark-skinned girl? High-spirited?" Salut said. "I remember her. She came in here three days ago and started shouting, demanding to speak with the man in charge. We're not used to seeing women like that around here. . . . I mean, even though her clothes were ragged, she seemed like a decent girl, know what I mean? I suppose that's why I remember her so well."

"What happened then?"

"We told her everything we knew. That you'd come in here, that you'd left at nightfall, and that we hadn't seen you since." He looked Walid up and down. "I can guess what happened to you. A rough encounter with the wrong sort, eh?"

"What did she do?" Walid went on, ignoring him.

"She left the way she came, of course. Women ought to wait for their men at home. If they go out and act on their own, they're bound to get in trouble, know what I mean?"

Walid was in no mood to listen to Salut's advice. His only concern was to find Zahra right away. While he settled back into the house of Mr. Raschid, Karim tried to find out whatever he could about Zahra. He and his men asked all around the city, but had no luck. It was as if the earth had swallowed her up.

"By now, Malik, all of Damascus knows you are looking for her," said Karim. "If she's still in the city, she will hear about it too."

Walid did not let himself lose hope. As soon as he could walk with the help of crutches, he roamed Damascus in search of Zahra. But when it was clear that he would not find her, a deep sadness fell on his heart. He spent several days in the kitchen, sitting by the fire, hardly eating or talking with anyone. At last, Karim said:

"Malik, you've been here for four months. It's not that we're tired of having you here, but surely, by now, people somewhere must be missing you."

Walid doubted it. Karim must have read this in his eyes, because he added:

"In any case, you ought to decide what you're going to do with your life. I can't stand to see you like this; I'm not about to watch a man just let himself die."

Walid looked at his friend and considered his words. Karim was right; he couldn't give in to sadness. He had lost Zahra, but surely she had gone back to her people in the desert. There was no reason to believe that anything bad had happened to her. He could go on with his search, and as soon as it was done, he would return to her.

But Hammad's wondrous carpet seemed farther away than ever. He had lost Hakim's trail, he had no money, his camel had disappeared with Zahra, and he could not even walk without a cane. He recalled what a poet once said — "When complaining does no good, patience is the better road" — but he could not help but feel discouraged.

"I have nowhere to go," he told Karim wearily.

"Then perhaps you should stay with us," the man answered. "I am sure there would be a place for you among the servants."

Walid understood what Karim was saying; he had spent four months living under this roof, and hospitality had its limits. But something inside him rebelled against working for someone else. He had been a prince, a king, a thief, a herder of camels. He had never taken orders from anyone. Even among the Bedouins, he had been his own master. He would gladly have paid for his room and board, but he had no money.

"Don't worry," he said to Karim. "I will go in the morning."

"And where will you go? You said yourself that no one is expecting you anywhere."

Crippled and penniless as he was, Walid had to admit that he would not be good for much. He struggled within himself, but finally said: "All right. I'll join you as a servant. Tell me what I should do."

* * *

Since he couldn't walk without a cane, he was given tasks he could perform sitting down. Some of these didn't bother him — they were the kind of chores he had done among the Bedouins — but others struck him as women's work, and he had not been brought up to do that sort of thing. Yet then he remembered Zahra, whom he considered his equal, his companion, his other half, and wondered whether he wasn't being unfair to belittle the work she used to do among the clan. What's more, Zahra had been able to do plenty of the men's jobs — better than some of the men Walid had known.

And so he ended up accepting any kind of work, hoping in this way to repay the debt of gratitude he owed to Mr. Raschid, the owner of the house, whom he had not yet seen. As far as he could gather, the man was often traveling, and didn't spend much time in his house in Damascus.

The months passed slowly. Walid's legs continued to

heal, and soon he began to earn wages, since there were no slaves in the rich man's house, but only free men who were paid for their work. Eventually Walid was able to save up some money. As soon as he saved enough to buy a camel, he planned to return to the Bedouins to find Zahra. In the meantime, he kept inquiring into Hakim's whereabouts. But he had no luck.

In Raschid's house, he was able to exchange his threadbare *djellabah* for a newer one, plain and simple enough but clean. He learned what it was like to work in a fine house and to see its wealth from another perspective. He avoided all jealous talk and plotting, doing his work promptly and efficiently. He trusted Abla and Karim, but even to them he spoke only when he needed to.

And one day, the man of the house returned to Damascus. The usually quiet mansion became a beehive of activity and commotion. Everything had to be just right when Mr. Raschid came home. Walid took part in the preparations, but he had no interest in meeting the master himself.

Mr. Raschid departed again just a few days later, this time on a short journey of less than a week. One morning, Walid found Karim in a terribly worried state.

"That blasted Kafur," he grumbled. "He swore to me that he knew Hebrew. Now what am I going to do?"

He explained to Walid that Mr. Raschid had been waiting for an important message from some Jewish merchants. The message had arrived that very morning, and soon afterward, Kafur, Raschid's secretary, had presented himself before Karim, all flustered, confessing that he did not know the Hebrew language after all. Karim had dismissed him at once.

"Now what will I do?" the man groaned. "The boss is waiting. He told me to send him a messenger as soon as it arrived. Where will I find another secretary to translate it?"

"I can do it," Walid offered. "I know how to read Hebrew."

Karim was astonished, but Walid gave no further explanation. He simply translated the letter in his elegant, princely hand, a product of the thorough education he had received in Kinda, and returned to his work, quiet and circumspect as ever.

*   *   *

Days later, Karim came into the kitchen looking for Walid.

"The master wants to see you," he announced, looking at him with new respect.

Walid was not so eager to meet the man whose servant he was, but he got up and followed Karim, limping and leaning on his cane.

12

THE MERCHANT

Mr. Raschid was a striking man with a thick beard and friendly blue eyes, and as Walid entered the room, the man's smile revealed two rows of gleaming white teeth.

Walid paused a moment before him, then hurried to bow reverently as he had seen his own servants do in Kinda. His slow reaction did not pass unnoticed by Raschid, who raised an eyebrow and studied him curiously.

"I have the impression you are not a man accustomed to obeying orders," he observed.

"Pardon me, sire; I am a simple man of the desert," Walid said. "But I will grow used to it in time. I haven't served very long yet in this house."

"Four months and twelve days, to be precise," Raschid replied. He laughed at Walid's flustered reaction, and added gaily, "What kind of master would I be if I didn't know what went on in my own house? I know your story: They call you Malik, and barely two days after you came to Damascus you were attacked by thieves who would have killed you if my good man Karim hadn't happened along. Your legs were broken and you spent some time recuperating under my roof. Now you work for me, hoping to earn enough money to go searching for the beautiful young girl you lost. Am I right?"

"Yes, sir."

"Very good, very good." Raschid held him with a thoughtful gaze. "I know the pride of desert men, Malik, and I can understand how hard it must be to find yourself taking orders from a stranger. Yet I also know you are no ordinary Bedouin. I suspected as much from the start, but not long ago I received something that confirmed my suspicion."

Raschid held up a scroll that Walid recognized at once: his translation of the Jewish merchant's message.

"Tell me, Malik: How many languages do you speak?"

Walid told him, and as he described his knowledge, Raschid shook his head in amazement.

"Clearly, you are no everyday tribesman."

There was no harm in telling only half the truth, Walid supposed.

"I was raised in a royal court," he explained, "but there were troubles, and I had to leave the palace."

"To join up with Bedouins?" Once again Raschid raised an eyebrow, and Walid did not answer. "I suppose that if you're in some kind of trouble with the law, you're not going to tell me," Raschid sighed. "Very well. I'll take my chances."

He leaned toward Walid with a conspiratorial look. "I'll come right to the point, Malik: Would you like to be my secretary?"

Walid was startled by the sudden turn of the conversation.

"I can well understand that a man of your background and education would aspire to something more than stirring pots in a kitchen," Raschid added. "As my secretary, you would earn better pay and you wouldn't have to lodge with the servants. Think about it: It's a very good offer."

Walid said nothing. The proposal was a tempting one, but to accept it would mean attaching himself even more firmly to Raschid and his house. . . .

"To be honest, sire, you wouldn't be able to count on my services for long," he said. "I have been planning to leave Damascus as soon as I'm able."

Raschid nodded thoughtfully.

"But at least I could have you at my side until I found another secretary."

When Walid failed to answer, the merchant looked at him askance.

"You're a man of few words, aren't you?"

"At one time I was more eloquent, but it only brought

me trouble," Walid said with a shrug. "I propose the following, sire: I will be your secretary until circumstances permit me to leave your house and continue on my way."

Raschid let out a deep sigh. It seemed he was going to say something more, but he held his tongue and sighed again.

"Agreed," he said at last. And so Walid ibn Hujr, the Wandering King, became the secretary of the rich man Raschid.

* * *

Walid soon realized that Raschid was one of the most powerful merchants in all of Arabia. He owned several caravans that traveled, as he liked to say, "as far north as Syria and Palestine, west to Egypt, east to Persia and Babylonia, and all the way to Yathrib, Mecca, and Yemen in the south." Yet none of his caravans crossed central Arabia, where the proud kingdom of Kinda had once been.

At first, Walid performed his duties without leaving Damascus, but Raschid soon began to ask for his company on short journeys to neighboring cities. Walid still resisted accompanying him on any large-scale travel; while he hoped Zahra had returned to the Bedouin's, there was always the chance she might still be in the city, and at any moment she could hear where he lived and appear at the house. Raschid did not insist, but Walid knew that sooner or later he would have to travel as the job required of him. That moment arrived one morning in spring, when Raschid unfolded in front of his secretary a map of the route his next caravan would follow.

"The festival of Mecca," he announced with satisfaction. "A good occasion for selling the silks I brought from the Orient, and for buying incense and myrrh at a good price. See how the route goes: Sakaka, Tayma, Yathrib, Mecca. A long journey. I believe I will need your help in negotiating. . . ."

"Sakaka?" Walid repeated, suddenly with great interest.

He studied the map again while making quick calculations in his mind: If he wasn't mistaken, this was the time of year when the tribe of Sheik al-Harit liked to camp between al-Gandal and Sakaka, in an oasis that appeared to be marked on the caravan route. It would be a perfect opportunity to find out whether Zahra had returned home to her people.

"I will go with you," he said without hesitation.

The caravan left Damascus one week later, an immensely long line of camels packed with riches and guarded by warriors. Various small tradesmen had brought their camels together in Raschid's group, paying him in order to travel with a large caravan and benefit from its protection.

Walid felt impatient at first, because the caravan

advanced so slowly. He had been accustomed to flying over the dunes on the back of a horse or camel, the wind beating in his face, and he could not get used to the exasperating slowness of the endless columns of animals. Yet he tried to relax, to enjoy something of the ride from high on his camel.

It was more difficult than he expected. The long days of travel under the blazing sun became interminable, and he couldn't help but ask himself whether it had been a good idea to leave Damascus, where he had seen Zahra last.

Raschid, on the other hand, was always good-humored.

"There's nothing better than the life of a caravan merchant," he told Walid. "To travel, to see the world, to meet interesting people, and best of all, so many possibilities for getting rich! I started out with very little money. I bought two camels and joined a great caravan going to Palmyra. With the money left over I took along a small cargo of fine silks. They told me I was mad, that I needed something more secure, like joining one of the caravans on the incense route. . . . But I arrived at the festival of Ukaz before everyone else did, and I sold my silks for the price I wanted."

Raschid went on talking exuberantly, and Walid listened, grateful to have some kind of diversion, until finally, after ten days, they came within sight of the oasis.

His heart beating fast with excitement, he followed the caravan's slow pace until it halted just outside the little grove of trees. He let his camel go over to the stream to drink, then got down and walked through the oasis as quickly as his legs would allow. But suddenly he stopped. The Bedouins were no longer there.

Walid searched the oasis again, his heart breaking, and found some traces of evidence that the tribe of al-Harit had stopped there — the remains of a deer enclosure, ashes from the fires at night, even a scrap of a woman's clothing caught in a tree. Walid could not help but think of Zahra. He explored on and saw that the river carried less water than he remembered, and that many of the trees were withering. It was evident that drought had parched the pastures, and so the Bedouins had moved on before the end of the season. And in the vastness of the desert, there was no way to know where they could have gone.

He returned to the caravan, downcast. Raschid was eating dates at the foot of a palm tree, and understood the situation with one look at his dejected face.

"Good material for a *nasib*, isn't it?"

"What do you mean?"

Raschid gestured around him. "The poet arrives at the camp of his beloved's tribe, but they have gone away. Isn't that the theme of the *nasib*, the first part of the *qasida*? I thought all Bedouins were poets."

"I don't feel like writing any verses at the moment," Walid said angrily.

"Maybe not," Raschid admitted, "but maybe one day you will compose a *qasida*, and then you will remember this."

Again Walid thought of al-Nabiga al-Dubyani, the great poet who had bestowed victory on Hammad ibn al-Haddad, so long ago.

"Look on the bright side," Raschid added with a shrug. "Imagine for a moment that the girl has not come home. You've saved having to explain to her father that you lost all trace of her."

"I don't see any advantage in that," Walid replied. "What's certain is that I have lost her, and it does no good to shirk my responsibility. It's my fault. I should have taken care of her."

"Is it your fault you were attacked in an alleyway? You have a strange sense of responsibility, Malik. Men make mistakes. If we were held accountable for every one of them, we'd never be able to hold our heads up for the rest of our lives."

Walid shook his head and said nothing.

At dawn the caravan went on its way. Walid was silent and sad, and not even Raschid's animated conversation could shake him from his self-absorption. Soon afterward, they arrived in Mecca. Walid had never felt particularly drawn to the world of the caravans; neither the festivals nor the caravans themselves had attracted his interest as a child. Yet in Raschid's company he became immersed in the festival atmosphere, and let himself catch the fever of trading and selling, amazed at the endless wealth of silks and spices. Soon he joined Raschid in his business dealings and discovered his own talent for the work, so that on more than one night they ended up drinking in a tavern to celebrate the conclusion of some profitable trade. When they returned to Damascus, the camels loaded with the finest incense of Nagran, Walid guessed that he would accompany Raschid on many more journeys.

*　*　*

Months passed. Walid's legs recovered so that he barely needed to use a cane, and his earnings increased. Yet he had been putting off his search for the carpet indefinitely, and Raschid had done nothing to find a new secretary. For his part, Walid had come to truly appreciate the man. He admired his inner strength, his good humor and generosity, and he was grateful for everything Raschid had done for him. If Karim had saved his life in that narrow street, Raschid had revived his spirit. Not only had he trusted him on blind faith, but he had given him work when he could not even walk, and then had made him his secretary, placing the younger man directly at his side. Having worked for him for some time now, Walid felt he had regained the ability to laugh.

"Your generosity is great, sir," he said one day. "You deserve to have not just a *madih* but a whole *qasida* dedicated to you."

"Nonsense, Malik," Raschid replied with his usual bluntness. "I don't need a swarm of hypocritical flatterers buzzing around me like flies, reciting nauseating verses full of lies and false praise."

Walid did not answer, but he thought about Raschid's words for a long time. He realized with surprise that he *wanted* to compose verses in honor of Raschid, his master — that such verses could burst freely from his heart. But perhaps for fear of disappointing the merchant, he didn't let any of them escape his lips.

Raschid soon discovered that his servant was a master at bargaining, and he gradually allowed Walid to become more and more involved in the business. The eloquence Walid had displayed in his youth as a prince, diplomat, and poet had many uses; among the Bedouins, Walid had been a major force in their dealings with other tribes, but for Raschid, he became a dependable key to success in all his affairs.

"And here, I thought you were a man of few words!" Raschid liked to say.

Thanks to Walid, the merchant's earnings multiplied

in such a way that one day he proposed making Walid his partner — an offer Walid did not refuse.

Together they traveled throughout Arabia along the caravan routes. Walid came to know everything that the great cities had to offer, and he learned to appreciate the desert from a new perspective. Nevertheless, in every new city he came to he sent his servants to find out whether a certain Hakim, a *rawi* and a thief, had been there — or a Bedouin girl named Zahra, beautiful as a desert flower. And he asked for her whenever he and Raschid returned to Damascus.

"I'm reassured to know that you're still as obsessed as ever, even with your comfortable new state in life," Karim teased.

It seemed strange to Walid to think that Karim and Abla could compare him with his master, Raschid. He saw that he did not like being placed above other people, and he recalled his days as a prince. He had had dozens of servants, but had never really known any of them. They could have been people like Karim, or Abla, or even Hammad. Simple folk, but human beings just like him. Yet he would never know.

So he tried to make it clear that, even though he had become the powerful merchant's new partner, nothing would change his relationship with the people who had saved his life months before in a dirty alleyway of Damascus.

✲   ✲   ✲

One day, nevertheless, his luck changed in a surprising way.

He and Raschid found themselves in Hegra, preparing to send a caravan toward Oman. As they strolled through the bazaar, enjoying a couple of leisure hours, Walid thought he could see a familiar figure in the distance. It was only for an instant, but it seemed to be that mysterious old man in the red turban, whom he had come across twice in his travels at such unlikely places and times.

Without even thinking, he set off through the crowd, his heart beating madly, eager to get to the bottom of this mystery. The bazaar was full of people, but even so, Walid was able to catch sight of the little man several more times, just farther ahead, always a little bit farther, until finally he disappeared.

Walid stopped, tired, leaning on his cane and cursing his luck. If those thieves hadn't broken his legs, he would have been able to catch up with that enigmatic man and find out . . .

Suddenly, something — a strange impulse, an inaudible voice whispering in his ear, an intuition too powerful to ignore — told him to turn his head, and without thinking, he obeyed. A short person beside him had slipped a hand into his pocket, silently as a cat.

In a flash, Walid reached out and grabbed the thief, who let out a stifled cry. Walid saw that it was a girl, but

[163]

felt no compassion. He knew that thieves were often murderers too, and this young woman could have killed him on the slightest impulse, like the ones who had attacked him in Damascus.

"Do you know what the punishment is for robbery, little thief?" he asked in a voice loud enough for others to hear.

The girl tried pleading:

"Powerful master . . . take pity on me. . . . I have twelve brothers, my father died, and my mother is sick. . . ."

Walid shook his head in surprise — not because he believed the girl's worn-out story, but because her voice . . .

And taking advantage of this moment of hesitation, she freed herself with a sudden jerk and started running.

"She's escaping! Stop her! Thief, thief!" people cried. Their voices brought Walid to his senses, and he called out with all his might:

"Zahra!"

The girl stopped suddenly a short distance ahead and turned to face him. She was as pale as if she had seen a ghost. Her lips formed Walid's name, and she ran toward him instantly, just before a few men who were trying to capture her could reach her.

They met in a long and passionate embrace.

Disappointed that they were not going to get to punish the thief, the crowd returned to its affairs, and life went back to normal in the Hegra bazaar. Only Zahra and Walid remained still, embracing for a long time, until she pulled away from him and began to dry her eyes. Beneath her dirty face and the ragged men's clothes she wore, she seemed to Walid to be a more mature woman now — but her beautiful eyes shone the same as when he had first seen them.

"Oh, Walid," she sighed. "I've looked for you everywhere. I thought you were dead."

"And I have looked for you, Zahra. I thought you had returned to your people."

"And abandoned you?" She sized him up with a glance, a teasing sparkle coming into her eyes. "But I see that you have not done badly without me. I, on the other hand . . . you can see for yourself that I've had to steal to stay alive."

It was not a reproach, but Walid felt guilty.

"You will never do it again," he promised. "I am a rich man now, Zahra. Stay by my side and you will become a queen."

"But what about the carpet?" she asked.

Walid gave her the same excuse he had been telling himself all this time:

"I am looking for it. As a merchant, I travel often, and everywhere I go, I make inquiries. I search all the markets and bazaars, and I examine every carpet I see. So far I have had no luck, and without further clues, there's nothing more I can do."

This argument seemed to half convince her.

"Come," Walid said, taking her by the hand. "I will take you to the house of my partner, my friend Raschid. He will be very happy to meet you, because I have spoken of you so often."

Zahra looked at him doubtfully, then looked at herself. Her clothing was tattered and her hands were dirty.

Walid understood. "Don't worry," he told her. "It doesn't matter what you are wearing. Your beauty will shine through."

*   *   *

Raschid's house in Hegra, considerably smaller than his headquarters in Damascus, was nonetheless equally comfortable and luxurious. Walid left Zahra with the servants and went off to tell Raschid the good news. He found him strolling in the garden.

"Raschid, you won't believe it," Walid began in a rush. "I have found Zahra here in Hegra." And he told him all the details of their encounter.

"By all the *djinns*, this is something to celebrate," laughed Raschid. "I hope she will accept my hospitality. You know you are both welcome in my house."

"I truly thank you, Raschid." Walid suddenly became sober. "I will never be able to repay you for everything you've done for me."

"I divide my earnings with you, and even so, I have more than I did before you worked with me," Raschid replied. "Good heavens, Malik, you owe me nothing. I am the one who should be grateful to you."

They both knew that Raschid was exaggerating, and therefore Walid felt it necessary to insist:

"No, really, Raschid, why did you save me? If you go around involving yourself with every wounded beggar you find in the street, you'll end up in ruin."

Raschid laughed again. Walid had learned that it was easier to talk to the merchant about serious things if they were said half in jest.

"Well, first of all, I didn't save you. Karim did. He knows that everyone is welcome in my house, even the poor." His face darkened. "Especially the poor, if they are honorable. I have never forgotten that I was once poor myself."

"You were? You've never told me that. You told me you began with two camels. . . ."

Raschid smiled.

"True enough. I began with two camels, but before that, I had nothing. My family was poor. My father served various masters until he was able to establish himself and marry my mother. We wandered a long time before finding what seemed to him the best place to live — a village lost in the middle of nowhere, and yet he liked it. Perhaps because he had once gone hungry, he was resigned to living a simple life, earning just enough to get by. He considered it a blessing. My parents were happy, and my brothers were too small to complain, but me — I yearned for something more."

"And you've achieved it. Your father must be proud of you."

"I don't know. It's been years since I have heard from him. I imagine he's still in his village, but I haven't managed to organize a caravan to pass that way. No one goes to Kinda anymore. Perhaps I should . . ." He paused, seeing that Walid had turned pale. "Is something wrong, my friend?"

"No." Walid tried to smile. "Kinda is my homeland too. You really lived there?"

"Yes, in a dusty little village named al-Lakik. It was not a very promising place to start a business, so my father presented himself at a poetry competition and won, and gave me the prize money so that I could go to Palmyra. . . ."

Walid had to lean on his cane because his legs were trembling.

"Raschid ibn Hammad," he whispered. "I should have guessed it. What kind of work did your father do?"

"He was a carpet weaver. What's the matter, Malik?"

Walid fixed his dark eyes on him. "I have some bad news, Raschid," he said, half choking. "I am sorry to say that your father died more than five years ago."

13

THE BLIND MAN

Walid found Zahra in the entrance hall, freshly bathed and dressed in a simple linen tunic. She approached him with a smile, but her expression changed when she saw the look on Walid's face.

"What's the matter?"

"We have to go away, Zahra."

She asked no questions, seeing that he was too upset to speak.

Walid went to his room, took off his fine clothes, and once more put on his Bedouin cloak. He had earned a great deal of money during his association with Raschid, but he took only what he needed to buy a camel and provisions for the long journey ahead. His only desire was to leave this place, abandon the merchant's life, and go on searching for the carpet. Meeting Hammad's third son, it seemed, had been a sly trick played on him by fate — a fate that pursued him implacably, reminding him of his guilt whenever he dared try to forget it.

He said no farewells to Raschid nor to the servants, but simply went out to the street, followed by Zahra, and walked away.

He told her everything that had happened. He hadn't wished to tell the truth to Hasan, so as not to disturb the shepherd's peace, but he'd been unable to contain himself before Raschid, Hammad's eldest son. His friend had listened wide-eyed while Walid told the story of the carpet weaver and his final work.

Raschid had not believed him at first, but the look on Walid's face had been enough to shake his confidence. For his part, Walid felt so miserable that he couldn't bear to face him another moment. He had apologized and left as soon as he could.

Now he and Zahra walked aimlessly through the streets of Hegra.

"What will you do?" she asked after a moment of silence.

"I don't know. Go on searching, wherever I can." He turned toward her. "And you shouldn't go with me, Zahra. I'm cursed. I'm an unworthy companion for you or any other woman."

Zahra kept still, then said:

"I still believe that you are a good man. I believe that life will give you a chance sooner or later to amend your mistakes."

"Nothing will bring Hammad back to life."

"Hammad is more alive than you know. He lives in Raschid, Hasan, and Amir. I know Hasan, and from what you have told me of the others, I have no doubt that all of them are good men."

Walid pondered her words.

"But that still doesn't change the fact that Hammad is dead, and I killed him," he said at last. "I won't rest, I swear, until I find that carpet."

Zahra bit her lip pensively.

"Are you eager to leave Hegra?" she asked.

"Yes. Why?"

"Because I have an important matter to take care of here, but it won't take long. Can you wait for me?"

"What is it?" Walid asked.

"It all began the day you went off to speak with that man Salut and never returned. I was worried, of course, and after waiting for a good while I went to The Red Camel to look for you. They told me they hadn't heard anything of you since you'd left."

Walid nodded. He had known as much.

"But the next day," Zahra went on, "Salut came to see me at the inn, and brought a message from you."

Walid frowned. "He never told me that. Did he say that I was at the house of Raschid the merchant?"

"No." Zahra's eyes flashed in anger. "The liar told me you had gone to al-Hira because you'd learned Hakim was there, and that I should go to meet you."

"And you believed him?"

"Why shouldn't I? He gave so many details. . . . He told me your real name, that you were searching for a magical carpet that a certain Hakim had stolen. . . . What really surprised me is that you would tell your story to a rat like Salut, but how would he have known it otherwise? So I gathered up my things and left for al-Hira."

Walid could not get over his amazement. He trembled with rage.

"I never gave Salut any message for you. I couldn't have: They attacked me as I was returning to the inn, and Raschid's servants rescued me. I was unconscious for days, and when I came to, I sent someone to the inn to look for you, but you were gone."

"I had gone to al-Hira."

"Alone?"

"Alone. I spent weeks looking for you there, and when I was certain I had been deceived, I returned to Damascus to get even with Salut. The truth is, I never imagined that you could still be in the city; I thought Salut must have killed you, and that was why he had sent me far away, so that I wouldn't denounce him to the authorities."

"They almost killed me," Walid admitted. "Maybe they thought I *was* dead, and that's why they lied to you. But how did they know my real name? No one in Damascus knew it."

"I coaxed that out of Salut," Zahra went on. "There's nothing a man won't say when he has a knife at his throat — much less somebody who's more rat than man."

Walid marveled at her spirit.

"He told me he was only following orders from the blind man al-A'sa, the leader of the thieves of Damascus. But al-A'sa had left the city. I kept asking around, and his trail led me to Hegra — the opposite direction from al-Hira, where Salut had sent me to look for you. So I came here. Al-A'sa is a very private man, so I had to pretend I was a thief and learn the trade so that they would accept me into their society."

"You were taking a terrible risk."

"I wanted to avenge your death. At any rate, I only learned three days ago where this man al-A'sa is hiding. I was saving up money to buy a sword to cut off his head, but since you're alive, I will show him more mercy — though I don't want to leave Hegra without teaching him a lesson."

Walid nodded. "The pieces are falling into place. Salut must have told al-A'sa about the gold coin I gave him, so he sent his men after me. In fact, the thieves who attacked me seemed disappointed not to find more in my pouch than they did. So this was no random assault."

"Will you come with me to al-A'sa's house?"

"Of course. There are many more questions to answer."

After circling through dark and gloomy streets, Zahra and Walid stopped in front of a miserable hovel at the edge of the city.

"It's hard to believe that a king of thieves would live in a place like this," Walid muttered.

"He stopped running the gang some time ago," Zahra explained in a similar tone. "He lives here so he can go unnoticed, because he's still in trouble with the authorities. Besides, everyone says he's not quite right in the head."

Then to his surprise, Zahra stepped forward and tried to force the door open. He moved to stop her, but thought better of it and let her go ahead.

After several swift prods the door opened with a creak. At once a cracked voice shrieked:

"Who's there? Who's come into my house?"

The house was dark, but they moved in the direction of the voice. The filthy room held no more furniture than a straw mattress, some cushions, a rug, and a low table with a lamp that sent out a feeble light.

A figure cowered in the corner, a crooked skeleton covered in rags. To Walid he seemed more like a beggar than a king of thieves. Unlike most blind people Walid had known, including his own father, this man's eyes were covered with bandages.

"Who are you? What do you want?"

"We want revenge, you old liar!" Zahra cried furiously. "You've caused us nothing but trouble, and now you're going to pay."

"You're a girl!" the blind man exclaimed. "I don't know your voice, I don't know what you want from me. I'm just a poor blind man. Who's here with you? I can tell there are two of you."

"I'm a poor Bedouin who asked for some information in Damascus, and I received a cruel beating instead," Walid said coldly.

The blind man gave a start and trembled violently.

"You see?" said Zahra. "He remembers you!"

The blind man cowered even farther in the corner and hung his head as low as he could.

"I don't know you," he said, his voice choking. "I don't know what you're talking about. Go away, or I'll call for help."

"Who would help you?" Zahra snarled. She stepped toward him with her sword raised high, but Walid stopped her.

"Wait," he said. "I want to see his face."

The blind man hunched down farther still. Walid took up the lamp and approached al-A'sa, who moved back as far as he could.

Walid grabbed him by the wrist, and the blind man screamed and struggled. Zahra held him so Walid could shine the lamp in the man's face.

[175]

The light streamed over his features. Walid and Zahra had supposed all along that he was old, but he turned out to be much younger than they expected — maybe only a little older than Walid. Something had aged him prematurely: His hair had turned gray, and his long face, dominated by a certain fox-like expression, was withered and furrowed, as if some secret inner torment had taken years from his life.

Walid let out a muffled cry and nearly dropped the lamp.

"What's the matter, Walid?" Zahra asked.

It was difficult for him to speak, but swallowing hard, he managed to say:

"We know each other. It's Hakim."

Suddenly the blind man gave Zahra a shove and tried to run, but Walid grabbed him by his *djellabah* and threw him back into his corner. Al-A'sa moaned and whimpered:

"Please . . . master, my master Walid . . . take pity. . . . As the poet said, 'You have reason to reproach me, but a great man shows mercy!' I know we fought once, but I was a young man back then. I didn't know what I was doing. . . ."

But Walid recalled Hakim shouting to Masrur, "Kill him!" And he also remembered the conversation he had heard among the thieves who attacked him in Damascus: They seemed to have orders to kill him, orders that no doubt came from their boss, the blind man al-A'sa. Hakim.

"You lie," he spat at his old *rawi*. "You tried to kill me in Damascus too. Now I understand everything! Salut told you that a Bedouin named Malik was looking for a certain Hakim, and you knew that I had come after you!"

A disdainful look crossed Hakim's face.

"What kind of fool would go around calling himself 'king'? It was obvious!"

Walid struggled not to hit him.

"Where is the carpet?"

Hakim ran his tongue over his cracked lips.

"I burned it."

Walid froze, but Zahra said:

"He's lying. A rat like him doesn't know how to tell the truth."

"It's not a lie!" Hakim screamed. "For four years now I've been cursing the day I stole that hideous carpet! You don't know what you're talking about — you haven't seen it! That spawner of demons took Masrur's life and Suaid's sanity, and it made me go blind. Anyone in my place would have destroyed it too!"

"I'm sure this is a trick," Zahra replied. "Perhaps you're not even blind, and you're deceiving us about that as well."

"We'll find out in a moment," Walid said, and before

anyone could guess his intention he snatched the bandages from Hakim's eyes. The old thief cried out and covered his face, but Walid and Zahra had already seen the horrifying sight.

Hakim had no eyes.

"The . . . carpet did this to you?" Walid asked in a whisper. "Hammad too lost his sight, but not his eyes."

"I plucked them out myself to stop seeing such crazy visions," the blind man moaned. "No matter what I tried, the carpet would lure me and I couldn't help but look. . . . I tried to sell it, but no one wanted it. People would look at it for a moment and say it made them dizzy — they would get away as fast as they could. So I was left with it. I plucked out my eyes," he repeated, replacing his bandages, "but even now the visions torment me. They've planted themselves in my brain and won't go away. . . ."

Hakim started sobbing again. Walid could see that Zahra found the very sight of the man nauseating.

"Then you didn't destroy the carpet," Walid guessed, "because if you had, there would have been no need to blind yourself."

Hakim began to tremble, but composed himself at once.

"You have no idea what a man will do in a fit of madness!"

"You're lying. Zahra, look for the carpet."

She obeyed, appearing glad to be able to leave the room. Walid leaned over Hakim and studied him awhile.

"You vermin," he said. "What saddens me most is that once I was just like you."

"No, you were never like me," Hakim replied, and for a moment he recovered the cool manner he had once possessed back in Kinda. "You were a stupid young egotist. You thought the world revolved around you, but you never had the courage to destroy your enemies or the determination it takes to rule a kingdom. If you mistreated that old carpet weaver it's only because I told you to, but you couldn't even go ahead and kill him — you just set him to worthless tasks. You knew he was nothing but a poor devil who'd had the bad luck to cross your path. You don't have the cunning or the guts it takes to win, Walid. That's how you've always been."

Yet if Hakim was hoping to infuriate him, he failed. Walid observed him calmly.

"If having cunning, determination, and courage means being like you," he said, "I'm happy to have none of those qualities. But I don't think that you and I agree on the meaning of those words."

Hakim frowned disdainfully.

"If you hate me so much," Walid added, "why didn't you kill me when you had the chance, back in Kinda?"

"Because Masrur panicked, and Suaid had too many

scruples. We had to get away on foot. The thought of having left the king of Kinda unconscious terrified them. They were sure you would send the whole kingdom after them. Poor fools. If they had only known that the carpet would destroy their lives, that it had been created because of you, they would have killed you in an instant."

"I didn't force them to steal it."

"You deny responsibility for the misfortune it caused?"

"No. Nor do I deny my responsibility for the death of the carpet weaver and his wife. I grieve for them. I'm not proud of what I've done."

"That carpet weaver!" Hakim shook his head. "Your defeats as a poet were mine as well, because *I* was the one who recited your *qasidas*. I hated that weaver, and now I hate him even more for what he created, what it's done to me. . . ."

Just then, Zahra returned. "I couldn't find the carpet," she said, panting.

Hakim laughed. "What did I tell you?"

Walid looked thoughtfully at her, and then around the room. He spotted a dusty old rug rolled in a corner.

"Zahra, you were probably looking for some lavish, bright-colored thing, bordered with gold and pearls and precious stones. But often the world's greatest marvels wear a cloak of humility."

He reached out his hand, took up the old carpet, and

shook it a couple of times. When the dust had settled, the carpet still looked plain and ordinary, but Walid would have recognized its pattern anywhere.

"There is no doubt. This is the carpet of Hammad ibn al-Haddad."

14

THE ACCUSED

Hakim cowered as if he had received a hard blow, but suddenly raised his head again and seemed to fix his eyes on Walid, though he had none.

"Are you sure this is the carpet you're searching for?" he said coldly. "Look carefully; you don't want to make a mistake."

"Walid, no!" exclaimed Zahra, but it was too late. Walid had brought the carpet closer to his face to examine it by the light of the oil lamp. And he saw . . .

Beneath the layer of dust the capricious, bright-colored patterns that Hammad had created nearly five years before were entwining themselves over and over, around and around. . . . Just like the first time, Walid began to feel dizzy as the lines undulated and the forms spun slowly, then with increasing speed. He barely noticed Zahra, who had hooked her hand on his arm in distress, as he saw places, times, voices, faces, kingdoms, and wars, times of abundance and times of hunger, a handful of prominent characters and hundreds of millions of anonymous figures, all of them being born and living and dying, and once again being born and living and dying, in an endless cycle. . . .

"Walid!"

With great effort Walid took his eyes from the carpet and looked around, confused and mystified. Hakim's hovel seemed claustrophobically small after contemplating that maddening immensity. But Zahra's pleading eyes were as deep as a night without stars, and he held on to her steady gaze as if to a lifeline.

Hakim let out a choking laugh. "Go ahead, take it," he told Walid. "You won't have the courage to get rid of it, because your good friend Hammad wove it. In time you will end up like us poor thieves, going mad or blinding yourself or taking your own life. Because that is your punishment, Walid. Your sentence for destroying Hammad will be to carry that carpet until it destroys you. That is what your fate demands, O king of Kinda."

He uttered these words in a mocking tone, but Walid did not become angry. Instead, he turned pale, hearing his own sentence from the lips of this hateful *rawi*. *Hakim is exactly right,* he thought. *Fate has been pursuing me all this time, first when I was among the* suluk, *then with the tribe of al-Harit, then in the house of my friend Raschid. I've been unable to escape it. The carpet that destroyed Hammad will destroy me too, because that is what fate has written.*

He lifted his head and said, "Then I accept my fate, and my responsibility for what I have done."

Hakim raised his eyebrows, not comprehending Walid's meaning. But Zahra understood, and she looked at her companion in horror. Walid rolled up the carpet and placed it on his shoulder.

"Let's go, Zahra."

She cast a doubtful glance at Hakim, who continued to cower against the wall. Walid saw what was in her mind and gave her a bitter smile.

"I believe he has already gotten what he deserves. It's not worth our trouble to bother with him. Let the rat die in his own gutter."

She did not seem to agree, but neither did she object. In a moment they were on the street again. "What will you do now, Walid?" Zahra asked anxiously.

"Return to Kinda," he said, giving her a somber but decisive look. "I believe it's time to stop fleeing from my fate."

Zahra took him by the arm.

"There is no fate," she said. "There's no fate but the one we make for ourselves. All desert people know this. All brave men know it too."

"I will find out soon enough," he replied. "But for

now, Zahra, I must ask you to let me go, because what I have to do must be done alone. Go back to Raschid's house. He is a good man, he will take care of you — not that you need taking care of," he said with a little smile. Then his expression grew somber again. "I promise you that if I return, I will never leave your side again."

Zahra opened her mouth to protest, but the look in his eyes made her fall silent.

So it was that, standing still in the street, her heart sore and her eyes full of tears, she watched Walid leave her, perhaps forever, carrying the wondrous carpet of Hammad ibn al-Haddad.

✳   ✳   ✳

Walid bought a strong young camel and some provisions, strapped the carpet to the camel's back, and headed straight into the open desert. The journey was very, very long, but Walid showed no signs of fatigue or wavering. He traveled with his eyes fixed on the horizon and a glow of determination on his face.

After years of being away, he was returning to Kinda. He didn't know what he would find there, but this did not concern him. He wanted to see if there was something he could do for the people he had harmed — those who remained. When he had settled these debts, the matter of the carpet was all that would be left.

Before he found Suaid and Hakim again, he had thought that the best he could do would be to surrender himself and the carpet to Sayf — Amir ibn Hammad. But now that he knew the harm Hammad's creation could cause, he was no longer sure this was a good idea. He still had time to think this over, he told himself. But in the third week of the journey, something happened.

In the distance, he could make out what remained of the seven towers that had crowned the proud city of Dhat Kahal, the capital of the ancient kingdom of Kinda. Walid was headed in that direction when his camel became restless. He stopped and looked around, and saw that the sky behind him was turning dark, and a wind was rising that was stronger than usual.

"Sandstorm," he whispered. He looked around for shelter and, seeing a small hill nearby, spurred his camel on toward it.

But the hill seemed to be farther off than he had thought. Looking back, he saw that the storm was becoming an enormous cyclone of sand heading his way. He drove his camel as hard as he could, but he had the strange sensation that instead of advancing, he was going backward. The cyclone drew closer and closer. He would have sworn, if it weren't impossible, that the storm was pursuing him. He turned his camel to get as far away from it as he could, but the storm still headed his way.

Suddenly, something blocked the sun, and a mass of

hot air enveloped him. Walid closed his eyes as he felt the sand beat against his face. He dismounted and continued on foot, limping along aimlessly and covering his face with one arm, spitting out sand and leading his terrified camel with the carpet on its back.

He kept on until he could go no farther, stumbling and falling to his knees in exhaustion. The camel fled in fright, disappearing into the fury of the desert. Walid tried to get up but could not, anguished at the thought of losing his two greatest treasures — Zahra and the carpet of Hammad — so quickly again. He collapsed forward on the sand and lay there like a dead man. Then, suddenly, he seemed to hear a whisper amidst the thunderous roar of the wind — a whisper speaking his name. Walid lifted himself up to listen.

"Where . . . King Walid . . . ?" the wind seemed to say.

Walid shook his head to listen harder.

"Where . . . King Walid . . . ?" the sands moaned.

Finally he could make the words out clearly, spoken by a thundering voice coming from afar:

"Where are you going, King Walid ibn Hujr?"

Walid staggered to his feet. He saw before him a cyclone of sand, swaying in one place as if it were watching him.

"Where you are going, King Walid ibn Hujr?" this strange vision repeated.

"Who are you?" Walid asked, his voice sounding to him like the squeaking of a rat before a roaring lion.

The cyclone seemed to laugh.

"We are who we are," a voice behind him roared.

Walid turned and saw a second cyclone, and looking around he saw another, and another, and another: seven storms encircling him, standing in place and spinning. He trembled from head to foot.

"Djinns!" he said.

The *djinns*, the primal spirits of the desert, could help a wandering traveler on his way or drag him to his doom. They were wise, but they were also capricious and unpredictable. Now he was faced with no fewer than seven of them.

Walid wondered what he had done to draw the attention of these formidable beings, whether for good or evil. He knew that *djinns* could take on more terrifying forms than these, but also friendlier ones.

"What do you want of me, O powerful lords of the desert?" he asked.

All seven responded in a single voice, like the roar of seven storms:

"Where are you going, King Walid ibn Hujr?"

Walid cowered in fright. "I am returning to Kinda," he answered, "to finish what I began."

"And what will you do with the fabled carpet of Hammad ibn al-Haddad?" asked one of the *djinns*.

Walid hesitated. He had been asking himself the same question ever since he left Hakim's house in Hegra.

"I am not sure," he said carefully. "I have thought of locking it up with seven keys. I've thought of destroying it . . ."

Before he could finish, the seven storms roared with one voice:

"Fool!"

Walid fell to the ground, whipped by the fury of the storms, and buried his face in his hands.

"That carpet is one of humanity's most precious treasures," said the *djinns*. "And you dare to hide or destroy it, depriving the world of its magic!"

Walid did not answer. He too had sensed that this extraordinary carpet was an enormous gift to humanity, but after learning of Masrur's fate and seeing what had become of Suaid and Hakim, he had begun to doubt it.

"That carpet has destroyed the bodies and minds of everyone who has looked at it," he whispered.

"Fool!" the *djinns* cried again. "Those were impure souls who didn't deserve the knowledge they were offered. And you, King Walid ibn Hujr, have not shown yourself to be better than they."

Walid lifted his head from his hands.

"I am not worthy," he said to the *djinns*, overcome with guilt. "I know my faults, I recognize my errors. But I know that this is not enough. If I had been wise, I would have known that this carpet is a treasure. Punish me, lords of the desert."

"Look," said the voices after a long silence.

The carpet lay outspread before him like an eye of God.

Walid shuddered.

"It takes thousands of years for a human being to be born who is capable of creating a wonder like this," said the *djinns*. "Hammad ibn al-Haddad is proof that humanity contains something of the divine: the same power of creation that made the great marvels of the universe. It will take thousands more years until this creative power awakens within all mortal beings. Hammad ibn al-Haddad possessed a great soul, far ahead of his time. We *djinns*, the immortal forces of the desert, render him homage."

Suddenly the clamor of the storm ceased and a heavy silence fell over Walid, a silence so sudden and absolute that it seemed deafening.

Walid looked around. The cyclones remained in their circle around him, spinning slowly and silently. He did not dare disturb this sacred peace.

A time passed — he could not tell how long — before the voiceless voice of the *djinns* was heard again:

"King Walid ibn Hujr, listen to the *djinns*, listen and obey: Fix your eyes on the carpet and learn its great mysteries. The carpet will judge."

Walid swallowed and thought of Zahra, wishing

with all his might that she would find happiness with another. He had no hope of salvation now.

He rested his gaze on the carpet of Hammad ibn al-Haddad. He went over its perfectly intertwined lines and geometric forms, its complex and mysterious design. He saw it quiver and undulate, as if for the first time.

And before he knew it, Walid ibn Hujr plunged into the carpet's great secrets, navigating among thousands and millions of images, landscapes, faces, places, and times. At first he thought he was going to lose his mind, because everything was so jumbled together that it made him cry out. Yet slowly he managed to examine things one by one. Slowly he learned to look, not just to see. Just as Hammad had done in the archives of old Ibrahim, he began to classify the images into times and places, and he learned.

He learned the history of the human race. He learned what men and women had done in the past, what they were doing in the present . . . and, most surprisingly, what they would do in the future. That was the part he found most overwhelming at first. The things he saw were completely incomprehensible to him, and many of them contradicted each other. Sometimes he saw the same scene repeated with different variations, but without finding out which one was true. The past and present of the human race seemed ridiculously small before the sheer volume of images coming at him from the future.

It took him a while to understand that he was not seeing one single future, but innumerable futures, infinite possibilities.

Walid was transfixed. Losing his initial terror, he now contemplated these things with an inexhaustible sense of surprise. The carpet presented the future as a tapestry in which an endless number of different paths were interwoven, so that even though each path reached its own distinct end, each human being was free to decide which one to choose, whether to turn back, to follow, or even to open up a new path of his own.

Then is it just as Zahra said? Walid wondered. *There is no fate after all?*

He observed the carpet more closely still, and as he went over the pathways one by one, he realized that they often led to completely unexpected destinations, something unforeseen completely changing a person's initial decisions about which path to take. Yet it was also true that strength of will and devotion to one's dreams could lead a traveler where he truly wanted to go.

Walid discovered, too, that there were many kinds of travelers: those who knew where they were going; those who only thought they did; those who did not know and suffered because of it; and those who did not know and no longer cared. . . .

An infinite number of paths, an infinite number of people making decisions every day that could change their lives, that wove a future, an infinite number of possible futures.

Walid understood now that Hakim, Masrur, and Suaid had seen all these paths at once, and that their minds had suffered unspeakable things because of it. Then why was *he* able to understand the lesson in Hammad's carpet?

He tried to answer this by searching for himself in the depths of that magical, all-seeing eye. He saw himself die under the swing of Amir's sword, and he saw himself laughing with Zahra and their many children. He saw himself winning the poetry competition at Ukaz, and then he saw himself journey to far-off Cairo as a prosperous merchant. He saw himself as a prince, a poet, a tyrant, a king, a bandit, a Bedouin, a servant, a tradesman, and above all, as himself, Walid ibn Hujr. He saw that he possessed the strength to be what he wanted to be, and that Walid the tyrant had died some time ago, because he had not taken that path to its end, because he had turned back. . . .

And then he understood what Raschid had said about responsibility: He had committed a crime, but he was no longer the person he had been back then. He must try to repair his faults, but he must not let the weight of guilt pull him down or keep him from advancing on the new path he had chosen. For if he let himself be defeated by guilt, he would never have the strength he needed to reach the end.

He felt overcome by an immense sensation of relief, as once again everything began to turn and spin. . . .

* * *

When he opened his eyes, the first thing he saw was the torrid sun shining above him like a burning coal in the sky. He covered his face with one arm and turned about. The sand was very warm beneath him as he felt around, until his fingers suddenly grazed against something other than sand. It was the carpet.

Walid stood up, blinking, and looked all around him. He saw nothing but dunes. No longer could he make out the towers of Dhat Kahal in the distance.

He was in the middle of the desert, lost and alone. There was no sign of his camel, much less of the *djinns*. Only the carpet was at his side, stretched out on the sand, lovely enough but not especially striking for its beauty. . . . Just like any carpet one could find in any bazaar. But Walid knew it was still the wondrous carpet of Hammad ibn al-Haddad, and that having deciphered its mysteries, he could look on it now without fear.

Walid blinked again. Had it all been a dream?

"No, no, it was not," said a small voice beside him.

Walid turned around and stifled a cry of surprise: It was the little man in the red turban who had been his guide since the beginning of his journey. They were both in the middle of nowhere, without water, food, or camels, but the old man seemed cool and fresh as a blade of grass. He was not even sweating.

"Pardon me?" Walid asked weakly.

"I said it wasn't a dream." The man smiled in delight. "The *djinns* like to frighten people, but deep down they are good. I told them everything you had done, and they understood, as I did, that you deserved a second chance. As the ancient verses say, 'A man's true nature always shines forth, though he thinks he is able to hide it.'"

Walid was struck dumb with astonishment. Rearranging his turban, the little man said matter-of-factly:

"You have unraveled the mystery of the carpet because you have grown within, Walid. There are very few men like you. Not everyone is capable of learning, and growing, and seeing beyond themselves. Not everyone understands that they have the power to decide and to act, and most people who do understand do not accept responsibility for their actions. You are a wise man, Walid. I am proud of you."

Moved by these words, Walid could only say:

"Very well, I am glad — though it will do me no good now, because I'm lost in the desert."

"But haven't you seen your future in the carpet?"

"I have seen almost unlimited possible futures, but I

don't remember them. Nor am I sure I could remember a single image more."

"Your mind has forgotten them in order to protect you, Walid. If it hadn't, you might have gone mad. But everything you have seen has left a store of wisdom in your heart. Therefore you must know you have to keep faith in yourself and the human race."

Walid looked curiously at the little man.

"Who are you, anyway, that you know so much about me?"

He laughed gaily. "O great king of Kinda, everyone said you were inspired by the *djinns*. Don't you know that? I was at the head of your cradle when you were born. I am the *djinn* who watches over you."

And then the old man in the red turban disappeared.

*   *   *

Walid had limped along for several days with the carpet on his back when he saw a rider in the distance coming forward to meet him. He held still and waited.

The stranger stopped his horse beside Walid and looked down. His face was covered, but Walid would have recognized him anywhere. It was the *suluk* who once upon a time had been his best friend: Amir ibn Hammad.

"So we meet again," is all he could say.

"So we do," said Amir.

"How did you find me?"

"A strange man in a red turban showed me the way."

This news greatly troubled Walid; it meant that the little man who had claimed to be his *djinn* and protector had sent him to his death. Slowly he set the carpet down on the sand before him.

"Here is the final carpet woven by Hammad ibn al-Haddad. It is yours. And so is my life."

The *suluk* dismounted with a graceful leap and unsheathed his sword. But Walid made no move to defend himself; he stood calm and still and waited for death.

"I swore that I would kill you if you crossed my path again," the *suluk* said.

"I remember," said Walid, "and I accept my fate."

The other paused. "I hardly know what to call you. Are you brave, or are you now completely mad?"

"Perhaps I am both," Walid answered.

The *suluk* did not reply, but raised his sword above his motionless opponent.

Their eyes met, and in the horseman's gaze there was a steely flash that Walid knew very well. The sword blade shone a moment in the blazing desert sun.

Then Walid saw the sword descend toward him and sink into his chest. As he fell to the sand, clasping the bloody wound, his life passed again before his eyes. Once more he saw the place where he had been born and spent his youth: a high-walled palace in Dhat Kahal, the city of seven towers — a small refuge of green in the middle of a seemingly endless desert; the palace where his glory and legend and shame had taken shape and grown. . . .

* * *

Slowly, he opened his eyes and looked around in confusion. A tent billowed lazily above him; there was no one else present. He looked quickly down at his chest: He knew perfectly well he should be dead now, and yet there was not a single mark on his skin, as if the *suluk*'s sword hadn't touched him.

He stumbled to his feet and walked out of the tent. The desert sun hurt his eyes. Looking around, he saw that he was in an oasis that seemed familiar, though he could not quite place it.

His mind was a jumble of questions as he saw four figures on four camels, with a fifth camel behind them, galloping out of the desert toward him. He did not move. If they were merchants, they would help him; if they were bandits, they would kill him; and if they were Bedouins, they might do one or the other. He was at one of those dark places on the path where not everything depended on the traveler alone.

The figures became more and more clearly defined until they reached him at last.

"Greetings," said Walid.

"Greetings," they answered.

One was dark and lean; one was small and peaceful-looking; one was robust and jovial; and the woman had the most beautiful eyes that Walid had ever seen.

"Greetings," they said again, "Walid ibn Hujr, king of Kinda."

The travelers uncovered their faces. To Walid's astonishment, they were Zahra, Amir, Hasan, and Raschid: the woman of the desert and the three sons of Hammad ibn al-Haddad, the carpet weaver of al-Lakik. And the camel they were leading along — Walid would have known it anywhere — was one of his own, from the flock he had owned when he was a Bedouin. He had given it up for lost.

"I don't understand," Walid murmured. "Sayf," he said to the youngest, "you ran me through with your sword. You killed me to avenge your father's death."

But Amir shook his head.

"I didn't do it, though I nearly did. I looked into your eyes and saw something that made me hold back. You fainted and stayed unconscious for hours."

"But I saw you kill me!"

"In your mind, perhaps," said Amir.

A light went on inside Walid and he guessed the answer: He had seen in the carpet one of his possible futures, a future in which Sayf drove a sword into his heart. When Sayf had been just about to do it, Walid's mind had called up that vision, and it was so real that it had made him faint.

"I must learn to control these visions," he whispered, "to prevent this from happening again." He looked at the other three. "And you? How did you come to be here?"

"Zahra came to me in Hegra and told me about you," said Raschid. "She convinced me to come in search of you, and in search of my lost brothers." His face darkened. "At first I didn't believe her, but now I've heard the whole story from Amir's mouth, and I've seen the carpet."

Hasan smiled. "Raschid and Zahra came looking for me among the tribe of Bakr," he said. "I hadn't yet brought myself to go looking for my lost brothers as you suggested."

"I don't understand," said Walid. "How much time . . . ?"

"You were only unconscious for a few hours," said Amir.

"But several months have passed since you left Hegra," added Zahra. "Ever since then, we've been crossing the desert in search of you. Hasan and Raschid had almost lost hope, when this morning a strange little man told us where to find the fearsome *suluk* named Sayf, and he added that we would find you too."

"Now that you have found me," said Walid, still terribly confused, "what are you going to do with me?"

"We want you to be part of our father's legacy," Raschid said.

"Me? But why? What do you mean?"

Amir took something out of his saddlebags and showed it to Walid. It was a carpet — no, it was four small carpets, all strangely like Hammad's. It did not take Walid long to understand what had happened.

"You've cut it into four parts!"

"One for Amir, one for Hasan, one for you, and one for me," said Raschid. "That is how it ought to be, according to the law of the desert. This is the way to divide a father's estate."

"But I am not Hammad's son."

"More than you know, Walid," said Hasan. "More than you know."

"You need to understand: While this carpet may have begun as a punishment for our father, it didn't end like that," Raschid added. "We have seen it and talked about it at length, and we've understood that it was his last great dream. A dream he made real. Hammad wove this carpet, Walid, because he wanted to do it."

Walid looked at the four of them and thought about Hammad ibn al-Haddad. He had been faced with an impossible task set by an arrogant young man without half of his wisdom or heart. But rather than giving up or giving in to despair, he had reached deep within himself and created a miracle — a work of art that would last all the millennia it contained.

And then Walid understood. He understood that we often find ourselves at a great crossroads, at a moment when we must decide what we will do with our lives. That there is a path laid out for every person, but that only the traveler can decide if he will take it or not, and all along this path he has many more opportunities to abandon it. That if the traveler follows the chosen path to its end he will almost surely obtain his reward, though there are so many other paths, all of them leading to different places.

And that if he stayed true to his path, the path itself would thank him. That is why Hammad had managed to weave a carpet containing the entire history of the human race.

Walid took a deep breath, feeling a great measure of the guilt that had troubled him for so long lifting from his heart. Zahra led the fifth camel toward him and smiled.

"For you," she said.

As soon as Walid was mounted on his camel, he asked Amir:

"What did you see in my eyes that made you save my life?"

The *suluk* smiled.

"I saw my father," he said simply. "And I knew that he hadn't died, because he has gone on living in you, just as he lives in us."

Walid smiled too. And the five riders spurred on their camels and rode off together, toward the place where dreams come true.

Epilogue

THE WISE MAN

Like every other year, the poetry competition of Ukaz had drawn a great crowd of people to the entrance of the temple. One after another, the *rawis* rose to the stage to recite their masters' *qasidas*, and the judges listened and nodded and took down notes.

Among them was al-Nabiga al-Dubyani. He came every year to act as judge in the competition, but he had announced that this year would be his last. He claimed to have problems with his health because of old age, but only he knew the true reason — and he had not revealed it, for no one would understand. That reason was named — or had once been named — Hammad ibn al-Haddad.

More than ten years had passed since the final tournament in Kinda, but al-Nabiga could still recite Hammad's beautiful verses by heart. He had gone on attending competitions, hoping to see him once again, but he never did.

Now al-Nabiga al-Dubyani was tired of hearing poems that paled beside the ones he had heard in the mouth of Hammad ibn al-Haddad's son. No one but al-Nabiga remembered those *qasidas*, and this, more than anything else, made the old poet sad. And so he had decided that this year would be his last.

The day had been a long one, but luckily the contest was coming to an end, and the judges retired to deliberate.

"Pardon me," a boy suddenly said. "There is a man here who says he would like to participate."

"The competition is now closed," said one of the judges, but al-Nabiga held up a hand to stop him.

"Let us hear him," he decided.

He had a certain feeling.

And onto the stage rose a man with a determined air and a serene look on his face, his features hidden by a thick, dark, chestnut-colored beard. He was dressed very plainly — perhaps too much so for a great competition like this one.

The man began to recite, and the words floated over the plaza and into the hearts of the people gathered there. There was such tenderness and feeling in these words that women sighed and men knitted their brows, trying to hide the lumps in their throats. Al-Nabiga al-Dubyani fixed his gaze on this man, unable to believe what he had heard. Had a miracle occurred? He uncon-sciously crushed the scroll on which he had written his few stray notes about the other poets. *Nasib, rahil, madih*, the three parts of a *qasida*, perfect, bursting with love, mercy, tenderness, beauty, and above all, wisdom.

The man recited his final lines, and a brief silence fell over the plaza. Then the crowd honored the stranger with an ovation the likes of which had never before been heard in Ukaz.

The judges needed no time to decide. Al-Nabiga drew the stranger toward him.

"Who is your teacher, my friend?" he asked.

"Life itself, sir," he answered.

"Do you mean to tell me you have written these verses yourself? You have no *rawi* to recite them for you?"

"I still consider myself an apprentice, because every day I learn something new about the world. For that reason, I do not consider myself worthy to be called a teacher, much less to teach an apprentice myself."

And so al-Nabiga announced that this unknown "apprentice" was the poet who had won the competition. This time, the ovation was even greater.

"What is your name?"

"They call me *al-Malik al-Dillil*, sire."

"Very well. And what is your real name? It will appear beneath your beautiful *qasida*, because you have created a *mu'allaqa*, and your poem will be embroidered in gold letters and hung from the veils of the Kaaba."

"That is why I cannot reveal my name. I have not come here looking for wealth or glory, but only to follow a dream. I need nothing more."

Having said this, the mysterious poet waved in farewell and descended from the stage, and before anyone could react, he was lost in the crowd. The judges were indignant, but al-Nabiga smiled.

"We will write his name in letters of gold," he said. "So that everyone will know that the poem was created by the Wandering King."

He stood awhile, gazing into the crowd, and still smiling, whispered:

"Farewell, Walid."

* * *

The rider waited patiently in the dunes, under the stars, and before long another rider approached.

"I have made a dream come true, Zahra," he said.

She smiled. They both stayed silent for a while, contemplating the night sky, until she asked:

"Where will we go now?"

"Wherever we like, because anywhere will be my home if you are there."

She smiled again, but soon a shadow of doubt crossed her face, and she asked:

"There is something I don't understand, Walid. What was the reason for cutting the carpet into pieces?"

"Because for now it will do more harm than good, but there will come a day when the human race is ready to receive its message, and someone will come to reunite the four parts."

She looked at him doubtfully. "Did you see this in the carpet?"

Walid laughed.

"I saw that and much more. I also saw the carpet destroyed. I saw that we didn't divide it. I saw that we lost it forever. I saw that no one will find the pieces. And I saw that someone *will* find it, someone pure of heart. I saw that it will fall into the hands of unscrupulous people and a great disaster will occur. I saw many possibilities, but I dare to hope that one day it will all turn out as we wish."

Walid smiled, and won over by this hope, Zahra smiled too. She dug her heels into her horse's flanks, and it took off at a gallop into the heart of the desert. Walid gave a cry of jubilation and followed her. Then there was nothing but silence, and the light of the stars on the dunes, and the watchful gaze of the *djinns*, who never sleep.

Author's Note

The Legend of the Wandering King is a work of fiction, but some of the places and characters mentioned in it are real.

Kinda was a real kingdom that grew out of a coalition of Bedouin tribes in the late fifth century C.E. Some archaeologists say that its capital could have been Dhat Kahal, whose ruins have been discovered in south central Arabia at a place now called al-Faw. King Hujr, the last ruler of Kinda, was assassinated by the rival tribe of the Banu Asad early in the sixth century C.E. His son, Imru'l Qays, was a well-known pre-Islamic poet who went on to win the poetry competition held annually in Ukaz. According to legend, his winning poems, the *mu'allaqat*, were embroidered in gold letters on silk and hung from the veils of the temple of Kaaba, and he was later acknowledged by the Prophet Mohammed as one of the greatest of all pre-Islamic poets.

But Imru'l Qays's story did not end in Ukaz. Vowing to avenge his father's death, he successfully attacked and defeated the Banu Asad, then traveled from tribe to tribe looking for help in regaining his kingdom — thus becoming known as "the Wandering King." He even consulted the Byzantine emperor Justinian I, who agreed to supply him with troops. However, legend then says that the emperor sent him a poisoned cloak or put him to death by torture for winning the love of a princess of Justinian's family. Imru'l Qays died probably around 540 or 550 C.E., and his poems and journeys inspired the fictional character Walid ibn Hujr.

Another historical figure in the novel is the poet al-Nabiga al-Dubyani, also the author of a *mu'allaqa*, a panegyrist in the court of al-Hira, and a judge of literary contests, according to tradition. He lived after Imru'l Qays, however, and died in 606, so they would not have known each other.

The verses that appear in this book come from a variety of pre-Islamic Arab poets, many of them later in time than Imru'l Qays, and were taken from the anthology, *La poesía arabe clásica*, edited by Josefina Veglison Elias de Molins (Hiperión, Madrid, 1997).

All other events and characters described in this story are entirely of my own invention.

— LAURA GALLEGO GARCÍA

*W*ORD *L*IST AND *P*RONUNCIATION *G*UIDE

All terms are Arabic unless otherwise noted. The "ḥ" in Arabic is guttural, pronounced from deep in the throat.

agora (ah-gore-uh) GREEK   a gathering place, especially a marketplace in ancient Greece. The philosopher Socrates often taught in the Athens agora.

al- (el)   definite article, like English "the"

asabiyya (ah-suh-bee-yuh)   originally "spirit of kinship," often used in reference to loyalty to one's tribe or solidarity with a group

Bakr (bah-kur)

bint (bent)   daughter of

dillil (dill-ill)   wanderer

diwan (dee-wan)   a collection of poems that often functioned as a tribe's historical archive

djellabah (jel-ah-buh)   a full loose robe with a hood

djinn (jin)   a genie

fakhr (fahk-er)   a song or poem of self-praise, often substituted in place of a *madih* in a *qasida*

Hakim (ha-keem)

harem (hair-em)   a group of women associated with one man

Hujr (ho-jur)

ibn (**ib-en**)   son of

jahiliyya (**jah-hill-ee-yuh**)   literally "the time of ignorance," most
   often used in reference to the period of Arabian history before
   the birth of the Prophet Mohammed and the foundation of
   Islam (570–632 C.E.)

Kaaba (**kah-buh**)   a small stone building in the shape of a cube,
   located in Mecca. It was a center of worship for pagan gods
   during pre-Islamic times, and it is now the holiest shrine of
   Islam.

madih (**mahd-eeh**)   the third part of a *qasida*, which praises the
   poet's benefactor

Malik (**mel-ek**)   king

mu'allaqa (**moo-all-ah-ka**) (plural: *mu'allaqat*)   a *qasida* honored
   by being written in gold letters on silk and hung from the veils
   of the temple of Kaaba

nasib (**nah-seeb**)   the first part of a *qasida*, which customarily tells
   of the poet arriving at an empty encampment to find that his
   beloved has left

qasida (**kah-see-duh**)   a laudatory or elegiac poem in Persian or
   Arabic

rahil (**rah-heel**)   the second part of a *qasida*, which describes the
   poet's journey across the desert

rawi (**rah-wee**)   a transmitter of poetry; a skilled speaker who
   declaims a poem in competition

suluk (**suh-look**)   a bandit or tribal outcast

Walid (**wah-leed**)

Zahra (**zah-ruh**)

This book was edited by Cheryl Klein
and art directed and designed by Elizabeth B. Parisi.
The text was set in Centaur.
The display type was set in Poetica.

This book was printed and
bound at R.R. Donnelley
in Crawfordsville, Indiana.
The manufacturing was supervised
by Jaime Capifali.